She looked in the direction where he pointed.

Her face stared back at her from the giant stadium screens, mocking her as various emotions slid on and off her face. She issued a curse. Although no one could hear what she said, they could read her lips and surmise what she really wasn't saying—what the truck!

She turned toward Grant and pulled on his arm for him to do something. It seemed that anything she did caused an eruption of cheers.

"It'll be okay." He placed his finger against her mouth. "Shh. We can give them what they want and be done with it." He grinned as if he'd just won a prize.

Tamara blamed it on shock, otherwise she would have seen the kiss coming. But nope, her brain shifted gears, sending her body out of whack.

She had been leaning for her escape to the bathroom, so Grant only had to lean in slightly. His lips connected to her mouth with a gentle touch. She felt his partly opened mouth tentatively make its acquaintance with hers. Her desire unwound as if from a slumber, slowly swirling upward toward the surface with lyrical ease, issuing its own demands. She moved in closer. However, Grant released her lips and pulled away. The warmth that had suddenly departed was replaced with the cool air of the stadium. The crowd's roar blasted into her consciousness. She swore again. The heat of desire was long gone. Now her ears burned with embarrassment.

"We'll continue this later," Grant whispered. His gaze locked onto her eyes and then her lips.

Books by Michelle Monkou

Harlequin Kimani Romance

Sweet Surrender
Here and Now
Straight to the Heart
No One But You
Gamble on Love
Only in Paradise
Trail of Kisses
The Millionaire's Ultimate Catch
If I Had You
Racing Hearts
Passionate Game

MICHELLE MONKOU

became a world traveler at the age of three, when she left her birthplace of London, England, and moved to Guyana, South America. She then moved to the United States as a young teen.

Michelle was nominated for the 2003 Emma Award for Favorite New Author, and continues to write romances with complex characters and intricate plots. Visit her website for further information at www.michellemonkou.com or contact her at michellemonkou@comcast.net.

PASSIONATE GAME

MICHELLE MONKOU

HARLEQUIN® KIMANI™ ROMANCE

Hugs and kisses to Becky, Maria, Michele, Jenny,
Dacia, Kathryn, Annette and Tricia. Thanks to Schnee and
her team for creating Tokio Hotel America to gather and
nurture friendships.

Recycling programs
for this product may
not exist in your area.

ISBN-13: 978-0-373-86311-2

PASSIONATE GAME

Copyright © 2013 by Michelle Monkou

HARLEQUIN®
™ www.Harlequin.com

Printed in U.S.A.

Dear Reader,

As always, I'm thankful for your support. Whether this is your first book written by me or if you've been with me for most or my entire journey, I'm grateful. I can't believe that it has been over ten years since I received the call to purchase my first story, and now I've a total of sixteen titles. Your messages of encouragement inspire and continue to motivate me to keep those stories coming. Over that time, I have met some of you at various conferences and you are now part of my Yahoo Groups reader loop, Facebook or Twitter social networks. Again, I'm honored that you graciously spend your time and give support to my endeavors.

I'm also happy to share that I am working on a new series. A new family with a strong-willed matriarch, lots of drama and heartwarming romances set to arrive in 2014 and 2015. Stay tuned for the rollout.

While I thank my blessings, I'm mindful of the devastation wrought by Hurricane Sandy and Tropical Storm Athena in late 2013. Please continue to keep the affected communities in prayer and I urge you to support the various charities that assist with the devastation.

Peace,

Michelle

Chapter 1

As the sun rose, warm spring sunshine lit a widening path to the bed. Morning had arrived, bringing an end to another sleepless night for Tamara Wendell. She blinked repeatedly to lubricate her dry, stinging eyes. A wide yawn and a full-body stretch of her tight muscles did little to shake off the lethargy. But she knew that sliding farther under the covers to laze away the morning wasn't an option. She carried a vow in her heart that kept her going.

Her work at the New Horizons Leadership Academy had grown out of a dream to reach out to young men on the edge of tumbling down a path of self-destruction. Those young men needed her, and so she couldn't give up or slow down. Ever.

Emitting a loud groan, however, was still acceptable. Time to get up and back to work. She reached for

the stack of ten manila folders that had camped overnight at the foot of her bed. Each folder contained personal information about a young man considered to be
at risk. The sad and troubling details were seared into
her memory and, in each case, had taken custody of her
heart. Not only had she formed a bond with each teen,
but she, by way of the academy, had also taken on the
task to set them on the right path. She was proud of
her partnership with the administration of the Miller-
Brown Home for Boys and the grateful parents who
supported their work.

Every six months, she selected a group of guys from
the boys' home for the cooperative internship program.
Companies in the area opened their doors to provide
jobs and mentoring for the young men. If she couldn't
find them a job, the guys spent their time at her academy honing their computer skills, learning job interview techniques and participating in service projects
to develop a healthier self-image and confidence. All
the energy placed in rehabilitating them was to avoid
the alternative of becoming a part of Maryland's over-
burdened juvenile services.

As owner of New Horizons Leadership Academy,
her mission had a twofold purpose: not only to turn
around the destructive behavior and thought process
of these young men, but also to usher them into the
working world with a sense of independence and self-
reliance. Tamara jotted down a few notes on the writing pad near her lap. She always entertained creative
ideas that would benefit her clients. Most came to the
table with a "what is in it for me" mentality.

Thankfully, success stories outpaced the occasional

negative outcomes, solidifying her reputation in the community as a keen youth activist. Yet, the partnering of the guys to the right mentors didn't come easily. One company that she had in mind didn't seem to want to play ball. Benson Technologies had an internship program that was touted by colleges and universities, but when it came to opening up its doors to her academy, the welcome mat had been yanked in.

While a snooty human resources manager had the ability to block Tamara's initial approach, the executive didn't know the intense level of her tenacity. Some people had to learn the hard way. She was happy to declare that class was now in session. Ten young men depended on her.

Soft knocking at her bedroom door interrupted her musing. "Come in."

Her roommate Becky entered, a bit hesitant. "Hey, I brought you a cup of coffee."

"Becky, you don't have to keep doing this. But, thank you." Tamara took the steaming mug, savoring the robust scent. "Stop waiting on me hand and foot." They had been best friends for years and were now roommates.

"Can't help it. I made a large batch of coffee…and I mean large. That fancy brewing machine required a PhD." Becky offered up a rueful grin. "Plus it's lonely out there in that cafeteria-size kitchen. And can I say again that I'm really glad that you took me in?"

"Girl, please. I've crashed at your parents' so many times. Besides, it's not like you could stay in that apartment after your crazy roommate moved out. I told you not to sign a lease with her. Three jobs in six months, and that last one was a bit suspect, if you ask me."

"I'm not asking." Becky stuck out her tongue and made a face.

"Wouldn't you agree, though, that I've got more than enough room?"

"Of course! I'm in a penthouse." Becky's grin lit up her face, showing off her bright hazel-green eyes. Her honey-blond hair lay damp on her head and hung down to her shoulders in loose curls. She was still wearing her thick pink robe, and her feet sported matching pink bedroom slippers.

"Well, we have my dad to thank for that," Tamara said.

Before her father had passed from cancer, his sole goal had been to ensure that her mother and she were taken care of in every way. He had been an Ivy League professor, and his significant role in civil rights and his many academic accomplishments had made him a sought-after speaker and consultant on various commissions. His simple life soon exploded into a hectic, publicized—but very profitable—celebrity lifestyle. Tamara believed that fighting for human rights shouldn't be tied to gaining wealth, and that had always been a point of contention between her father and her. But he insisted that he had done the marches and protests out of his passion and his spiritual beliefs. So, she'd left him to do what he felt he had to do.

"Your dad died knowing that he'd provided for you," Becky continued. "Don't let that be tainted by your own crazy worldview that activism means you can't earn a living at the same time."

Tamara shrugged. Her guilt came from a deeper place beyond her father. But she hadn't ever shared the details, not even with her best friend.

"And can I say thank you again for letting me stay here for only four hundred dollars a month?"

"It would've been zero dollars a month if you hadn't pitched such a fit. I want you to save for a house. Stop paying rent—you get nothing at the end."

"There's no way that I wouldn't pay something. The place is the size of two apartments. I've never been a charity case, and I'm not going to use you like that. Although, if you loan me three quarters right now, I could buy lollipops from the vending machine later."

"You're such a candy fiend. Quarters are over there." Tamara motioned toward the top of the chest of drawers. "You know my mom picked this place. I was fine with a regular apartment."

"At least she talked some sense into you. People know your net worth anyway. Even if you choose to be dismissive, you are a millionaire."

She cringed over the word *millionaire*. The label felt like a heavy burden, given her desire to be a human rights activist as her parents had been.

Tamara sipped her coffee, enjoying the rush of the caffeine and its warmth through her body. With coffee mug in hand, she walked to the other end of her bedroom to pull out her clothes for the day.

"With that ratty nightshirt and funky-colored, mismatching socks, you certainly don't dress the part of a millionaire." Becky had carried her preppy look through college and now to the grown-up world. She embraced the Hollywood A-list, such as Reese Witherspoon and Anne Hathaway, as her fashion icons.

Tamara's own style was more chic casual, with T-shirts emblazoned with social messages, brightly colored jeans and athletic wear. She didn't have much of an interest in fashion icons.

Tamara looked down at her bare brown legs: not particularly long, but muscled from jogging and kick-boxing.

But she cleaned up well, according to the pesky fashion police on their gossip sites. Frankly, being termed a fashionista wasn't one of her priorities.

Today she had to fix that reputation…temporarily.

An idea that had percolated overnight had now taken hold in the brightness of the day. If she couldn't get what she wanted one way, then she'd try another method. She ran her hand over the clothes hanging in her closet. Picking the right outfit carried a lot of weight for where she planned to go and for what she intended to do.

"What's the deal with these?" Becky got comfortable in her bed. Sitting cross-legged in front of the files, she began flipping through them, occasionally sipping from her mug.

"It's still the latest group that I'm trying to get connected with companies. Well, one company in particular. But I've been kind of keeping it to myself because I didn't want to get anyone's hopes up."

"Any luck?"

"No. But when has that ever stopped me? I've got my eye on a computer game design and development company in Maryland—Benson Technologies."

Becky whistled. "The one in Rockville? Going for the big dogs."

Tamara nodded. "I want all ten guys placed there. They're a small company, but they're proving to be a powerhouse in the computer gaming industry. These kids would love that." She blew out an exasperated sigh. "But I'm getting the runaround."

"You know, if you mentioned your parents' bio with your introduction, you'd get past all the B.S."

Tamara didn't respond. Her thoughts raged over her need for independence and making her own path versus living off her parents' celebrity.

"You are hardheaded," Becky accused.

"Don't you have a job to go to?"

"Yeah, but the boss is out of the office. As a matter of fact, she's been standing in her walk-in closet for over five minutes now." Becky pushed back against the headboard and continued drinking from the mug.

"I'm trying to find the right outfit to go after Grant Benson."

"Is this his picture? He is a cutie." Becky pulled out a magazine nestled between the files.

"Probably used Photoshop. That was the bio picture on his website." Tamara was glad that she was partially hidden in the closet and away from Becky's eagle-eyed scrutiny.

The target, as she had dubbed Grant Benson, surpassed cute. The full-length photo had captured the computer gamer in a custom-fitted designer suit. The man had given computer nerds a boost in the hot-and-sexy department.

It also helped that he had the body of a model, with

broad shoulders, smooth dark skin and a slim athletic frame as well as the style of a classic Hollywood star. She'd already learned from various news sources that he was six feet five inches, didn't care a lick about basketball and was blessed with good genes that had earned him a comparison to a young version of the actor and activist Sidney Poitier. Although she admired the publicity photo, she'd withhold confirmation that he was gorgeous. She wanted to see him without the tricks of photo editing.

Was his skin really that smooth and was it the rich color of chocolate brown? Did those dark, piercing, almost black eyes have the same power to hold her attention if she was face-to-face with their owner? And what would his voice sound like? With a body and face that had the potential to weaken a woman's knees, namely hers, he deserved to have a deep bass voice with the smoothness of honey.

"Go with that burnt-orange dress. Shows off all your assets that you diligently work so hard to hide," Becky prompted.

"I'm not trying to sleep with the man. And my assets are nobody's business."

"Okay, let's see what *you* come up with." Becky turned on her side, propping her head up. "I was the one voted Best Dressed in high school."

"And that's because you baked cupcakes on the day of voting." Tamara walked through her closet, selecting each article of clothing, holding it up against her body, stepping in front of the mirror and switching items out to get the right ensemble. Once she had the right clothes, she flipped them over her forearm, grabbed her golf shoes and walked out of the closet.

"What is that outfit you're putting together? That won't help you to get young men to look at you."

"That's not the point. I'm heading to the country club to play a round of golf with Benson and negotiate a good deal for the guys." Tamara actually thought that she did look like a sports fashionista with her EP Pro Women's Monarchy ensemble.

"Love you for being so doggone crazy. But you need to bring it over to the slow lane and explain this strategy for me. What on earth are you doing?"

"Benson is a member of Parkside Country Club. That's no big secret. He's an avid golfer. I called yesterday to find out his schedule, and he's due to play this morning." Tamara dropped the clothes on the bed then air-swung an imaginary golf club.

"Don't you have to make reservations?" Becky asked.

"Well, see…you told me to use my parents' clout. And just this once, I did. Now, I'm in." She shooed Becky out of her bed. "Now go away, let me dress. You'd better head to work because you'll be busy after we book Benson Technologies."

"You're pretty confident." Becky paused in the doorway with both emptied mugs in her hands.

"No. More like determined. This is going to happen, even if I have to beat him at golf to get what I want." Tamara knew the nervous tremors in her stomach would radiate throughout her body when she actually had to go through with her crazy idea.

"Good luck, crazy lady. Don't get arrested." Becky left the room.

"I'll need a bit more than luck," Tamara said softly.

She headed for the shower with her mind already wandering to the possible outcomes. Under the cascading warm water, she practiced the speech that she hoped would get support for her guys' internships.

And, yes. They were *her* guys, as if she was their foster mother. She cared deeply for each teen. All the young men in her academy formed a natural, close bond with her and the staff. They were almost like the younger siblings she'd never had as an only child.

The connection with each teen who came into the academy bridged what she missed by not having a big family, but more important, it helped refocus her goal to be an advocate. More than anything, she wanted to work with young adults and to be an activist with the same spirit and determination as her parents.

Her strong desire to see the guys stay on the right path also made her protective of them and pushy about them seizing opportunities. Her loyal staff worked hard to keep their reputation growing and significant in the community. In this case, she wasn't going to pause in her efforts until all ten students had been placed with the right company.

Especially since the teens in this set were the diehard gamers of the academy. What a coup if she could get them into Benson Technologies. The hands-on experience in a top company would be invaluable. Plus they would have access to their dream jobs.

By the time she left her home in Tysons Corner, Virginia, the morning traffic had flooded the roadways for the early morning commute. Tamara expertly maneuvered her car through the city and out of the state to adjoining Maryland. Normally, she'd continue on the 495 Beltway loop toward the city of College Park to her academy.

This morning she aimed for Potomac, Maryland, the wealthy residential suburb where her parents lived and where Benson had an enormous mansion, one of at least three of his reported homes. She glanced in the rearview mirror, not only for the traffic but also to have a close-up check of her face.

She'd kept makeup to a minimum but didn't want to look too bare. A light dusting of foundation smoothed over her skin's almost invisible imperfections. Mascara and eyeliner had been applied with a deliberate touch for a sophisticated, rather than dramatic, look. She didn't like to worry about her hair and had opted to twist its length into a bun. Diamond stud earrings fit in each ear, their size and clarity showing off their value. The last touch was a light, coppery shimmer on her lips. All in all, she should be able to hold his attention long enough to get her point across.

Twenty minutes later, Tamara pulled up to the formidable security gate that allowed access to the country club's exclusive members and their playground. She was sure that, if she tried hard enough, she could detect a whiff in the air of the wealthy and powerful. The club's close proximity to the seat of power in Washington, D.C., and the nearby stately homes, attracted politicians, elite professional athletes, dignitaries and influential businessmen. After presenting her driver's license and club membership pass, Tamara drove onto the property. All around her was an overly green oasis of three hundred acres.

She parked the car herself, instead of valet parking, and retrieved her golf clubs from the trunk before heading to the main building. On cue, her pulse ratcheted its beat, matching her quick footsteps like background percussion. By the time she entered the cool interior of the building, her thoughts had fractured into various compartments of worries.

Panic soured her stomach. She gulped to keep down the coffee she'd had earlier. No time to deal with her weak stomach.

Suck it up.

How many times did she chant this as her new mantra? *Just about every day.* She would've liked to think that she had the spine for a few gutsy moves, but nothing about this situation was normal. If she couldn't get the company to commit to accepting the students, well, then, who knew what she'd be able to get for them? Definitely no other internship would engage them and guarantee their success like this one would. A compromise could mean the difference between a career and a life back on the streets.

Plus, compromising made her want to punch something.

"Good morning, Miss Wendell. How are you this morning?" The concierge greeted her with a wide, bright white, toothy smile.

"Fine. Um…can you tell me if Mr. Benson has headed out to the tee? Don't want him to start without me." She giggled to maintain her nonthreatening demeanor.

"Sure." Without hesitation, the concierge pulled up a screen on his computer tablet. "He hasn't checked in. But you're about ten minutes early."

"Great." Tamara pasted on a smile, but her lips trembled under the effort of acting like an empty-headed ditz. She headed to the private lockers to stash a few things before heading to the golf area.

"Tamara, is that you?"

Tamara turned and spotted the club's biggest gossip making a beeline in her direction.

"Hi, Mrs. Roberts. Yes, it's me." Tamara tried not to cringe.

"Haven't seen you around the neighborhood." Mrs. Roberts made a show of looking around her. "Are you alone?"

"I'm playing a round in a few minutes." Tamara hoped that the emphasis on "a few minutes" would have an effect. She didn't respond to the "alone" question. Mrs. Roberts liked to tell everyone that her children were all happily married to movers and shakers, and that she had the world's most precious grandchildren. Since Tamara scored a fat zero in both the marriage and children areas of life, Mrs. Roberts would always "tsk" with faked sympathy.

"I'll let you go, then." She tilted up her heavily lined cheek.

Tamara got close for the cheek-to-cheek kiss. She was too old to keep being the victim of Mrs. Roberts's sniping tongue. However, her mother would admonish her for not being respectful.

She heard the soft double "tsk" in her ear as she pulled away from the unwanted embrace.

"Please let your mother know that I'll be in touch. The Ladies Group is sponsoring a trip to Vegas and proceeds are going to the county library. We need to get more serious books on the shelves and drown out all those silly books about wizards and vampires."

"I'll let her know. But she is an avid reader of *those* kinds of books. She has tons of *those* books at her bedside. Tons." Tamara held her arms open wide.

Mrs. Roberts's shock was priceless. She knew that meant the busybody would call her mother and that her mother would bite the bait and call to chastise her. At the end of that rebuke would be more information about the latest wonderful thing that some Roberts's offspring had done.

Since her dad's death, her mother had become fixated with putting her on the fast track to marriage and motherhood. Maybe her mom wanted the comfort of seeing a baby born into the family. Thankfully, her mother wasn't the matchmaking type, although she had her share of nosy friends, such as Mrs. Roberts, to keep her mind on Tamara's lack of suitors.

Tamara turned on her heel and walked away from Mrs. Roberts. She rushed to the smaller clubhouse that catered to the serious golfers who didn't want to deal with the hectic buzz of the main clubhouse. Grant was bound to arrive at any moment. Sitting nearby would give her the advantage of sizing him up as he came into the building.

Besides what she'd read and seen on TV about the man, she didn't know much about him. Their paths had certainly never crossed at the club or any of his social or business gatherings. They traveled in separate circles.

Right now, that was a hindrance to what she wanted. But there was always more than one way to get the prize—such as dressing up for a golf game she hadn't been invited to play.

She ordered a soda and pulled out her phone to catch up on emails. But not even work held her attention for long. She couldn't stop thinking about the article she'd read that said Grant Benson had been a computer genius from a young age, excelling in high school, but that he had a brusque personality that earned him his share of enemies in school. Two years into a computer design major at the best college in the country, he'd left, armed with an early model of a successful computer game with more bells and whistles than she could appreciate. Major companies had offered to buy the design, but Grant had refused, earning criticism for his bullheaded stance.

Obviously he had known what he was doing because he'd gotten his financial backing that year, opened his company and never looked back. Now he competed with those same companies that had tried to buy his start-up. Year after year, he launched new innovative games and systems that created a cult following of teens and college gamers. Supposedly he liked riding his motorcycle when he was mulling over a project. Black T-shirts, black jeans and black tennis shoes were his standard getup. At an early age, he'd become vegetarian and gotten into yoga to stimulate his energy.

As for his personal life, she couldn't make a judgment. Not much had been written. Though she didn't give a damn about his personal dating habits, she couldn't help the small nudge of curiosity. After all, she had tracked all his other personal details. Plus he was too insanely gorgeous not to have women drooling over him. Only once had he been photographed with a supermodel. Rumors were that they were a serious item, but he got cold feet when she demanded a ring. Plus the prenup was a deal breaker for her. Neither one had ever confirmed or denied the rumors.

If the prenup rumor was true, Tamara almost felt bad for him. She had nothing against prenups, and she knew how money had the power to attract the bottom-feeders of the dating pool who didn't care one bit about you. Men seemed ever ready to fix on her material possessions or be intimidated by her personal wealth, and so she was always hesitant to date much.

Her phone buzzed and an incoming text popped in from Becky.

Becky: How's it going

Tamara: Waiting 4 him to arrive

Becky: OK let me know if he is sexy

Tamara: Don't you have work to do?

Becky: Doing it. I can multi-task

Tamara: Bye!

Becky: Details plz. Face. Body. His sexy-meter.

Tamara chuckled and set down her phone. Becky, the born romantic, saw most men as potential boyfriend material for her. Tamara had always thought it was silly.

At that moment, the door to the clubhouse opened and three men strode through the entrance. The leader of the trio definitely had alpha male qualities, especially with his towering height. He walked with a confident swag toward the hospitality desk. Tamara could see only his profile, but everything about him put her on alert.

The other two men were decent enough, but paled in comparison with the leader. He turned to speak to the men and she got a good look at his face. He was most definitely her target, Grant Benson.

Tall. Dark. Hot sex on two legs.

Lethal combination.

She swallowed a mouthful of soda, set down the empty cup and readied herself for the approach.

Chapter 2

With check-in complete at the registration desk, Grant surveyed the clubhouse. Still no sign of Simmons, his problem employee, and no calls from him or Latrice, his executive assistant, to give him any updates. Hopefully, no tragedy had struck Simmons, and it was only that the guy was as immature as he seemed to be. One would think that an invitation to play golf with the CEO wouldn't be treated as optional.

"We'll get started in a few minutes. Go ahead and store your things." Grant looked at his watch. "We've got a couple minutes." He looked up to find a woman staring at him.

"May I help you?"

"Um…I wanted…you. Talk." The woman hesitated but then focused on his face. "I would like to speak to you," she continued. Her scrutiny of his face momentarily muted him. His thoughts darted about. He wondered if she was someone he had once known or just another of those nosy reporters who were always trying to get an interview. Otherwise, there was no reason for her to check him out in such an intense way.

Either way, he was intrigued by the bold approach. His mouth hitched on the side with a slight show of his amusement. She sure wasn't hard on the eyes. Golf attire wasn't exactly revealing and sexy, but the color scheme of her clothes was sophisticated. The cute bangs feathered along her forehead capped her oval face while the rest of her hair was pulled back. Her medium build set her at about his shoulder, while her overall frame was an hourglass shape—curvaceous and feminine.

"Really." He muted his interest.

"Looks like you're in need of one more." She jutted her chin toward Hadfield and Norton, who were still browsing through the small gift shop area.

"Are you interested?"

"Yes, I'm interested. But before you think I'm a party crasher, I'm Tamara Wendell."

"I'm Grant Benson."

"I know."

He felt a frown deepen on his face. He scaled back his charm and replaced it with deliberate frost.

"I need to talk to you."

"Uh-huh."

"Your people are giving me the runaround." She moved her clubs closer to her body and struck a pose that was normal enough, except this beautiful woman standing in front of him defied normal.

"My people?"

"Your human resources department," she replied with an accusatory note.

"I have confidence that they know what type of person I need for the company's mission." He assessed her body. He wouldn't entertain any attempts to sway his authority over his HR department. No matter how pretty the reason.

"I'm sure they do. However, I didn't even get a chance to tell them about my guys."

"Your guys?" Now he couldn't beat back the curiosity. She was way too young to have sons who were looking for work. Maybe she was an overprotective sister?

"I run the New Horizons Leadership Academy, which helps young men. I link them with companies that provide internship opportunities, in addition to teaching them other life skills."

"Okay." Grant remained wary, although the request sounded harmless.

"Your HR department blew me off. Yet, you are known for having a robust internship program."

"Our interns work hard. It's not a charity program."

She visibly tightened under his crisp declaration. But he didn't care about her challenges. It was her job to make him care, and fast.

"I'm not looking for charity," she countered.

"This isn't the place for this conversation." He looked at his watch.

"You're right. So why don't we go play a round of golf? I'll take the brown-haired one over there for my team. We'll play, and if I get within a stroke of you, you will listen to me—with undivided attention."

"You're damned sure of yourself."

"Every second of the day." Again, she tilted that small chin with admirable determination.

He paused. Did his heart just hitch? Maybe it was that sexy scent that enveloped her like an intoxicating shield. Whatever it was, she had hit him like some sort of kryptonite, quietly and effectively crippling him.

He paused, took a breath and looked her right in the eyes.

"You're on."

Chapter 3

Whoever had invented the handshake to seal business transactions should be praised.

Tamara had shaken many hands as a business owner, but dare she say that this unique sensation was a first for her? When her hand touched Grant's to seal their bet, there had been an immediate response from her nervous system. How could a stranger's touch elicit such strong energy? She couldn't understand it, but she wasn't complaining, either.

Because really, what could cause the shake-up that now made her feel like a high schooler with a crush? Maybe she should stop looking into those hooded, dark brown eyes that seemed to shutter emotions from the world. Maybe she should stop admiring the angular lines of his face that were anchored by his square jaw. Maybe her gaze shouldn't hover and come to rest on his naturally pouty lips with a masculine wide flair. The man, physically, was the total package.

"Mrs. Wendell—"

"I'm just Miss. No mister in sight—not that I'm looking." She hacked out a hoarse laugh. "And it's Tamara. Friends call me Tammy or the Time Bomb. Well—" She quickly shut her mouth.

She felt herself blushing, and she couldn't believe that she had told him that her nickname was the Time Bomb. Now he probably thought she was a bit nutty with major personality issues.

The two men who had walked in with Grant finally made their way over to where they stood.

"Tamara, this is Roy Hadfield. He is my computer design specialist. This is Deetz Norton, my graphic design specialist."

"Nice to meet you." Tamara shook their hands, not worried that she'd have the same reaction with the two younger men. And she certainly was not disappointed when her response at shaking their hands was like a flat line on an EKG machine.

"You're joining us?" Hadfield asked. He looked over at his boss for confirmation. His clean-cut appearance and young face made him look vulnerable. Clearly, he cared what his boss thought, considering how carefully and measuredly he spoke.

"Yes. She'll be playing with Norton."

Norton looked as if he wanted to reject being her partner. Even though he didn't say anything, he gave a slight shake of his head. A red blush suffused his cheeks, adding another layer of vivid color to his ruddy complexion and his bright red hair.

"Problem?" Grant looked at his employee.

"Don't worry. We'll kick their butt," Tamara said, attempting to alleviate the tension with bravado. She didn't need the employees turning on her, especially since these might be the same men working with her teens.

"Sorry, I didn't mean to be rude," Norton muttered. He shoved his hands into his pockets and continued to look uncomfortable.

She playfully punched him on the arm and then leaned in close to whisper, "No worries. I know what a butt clencher it can be to spend the day with the boss."

He arched back to bark out a hearty laugh.

In a snap, the tension dissipated like a ghostly vapor.

They headed out to the parking area for the golf carts. Tamara figured that they must look like quite the colorful bunch, armed with sunglasses and toting the cumbersome golf bags.

Clouds gathered overhead in thick billowy shapes of white and gray. Their low presence appeared ominous despite the meteorologist's forecast of a sunny spring day. The crisp morning light was now muted, taking some of the edge off the rising temperature.

"Do you play often?" Norton asked her, his voice lowered as they walked ahead of Grant and Hadfield.

"Not really," Tamara hedged. Running the academy didn't allow for long hours on the golf course, or any-where else. However, once she'd settled on the idea of using the country club as the location to approach Ben-son, she had made time to practice. Back in the day, when she'd been in college, she had been an avid golfer. But she'd keep that little nugget of info to herself.

They teed off right on time. The game officially began with a couple of balls from the men heading off on a wayward slant. Slow and steady—her two favorite words—helped her. She swung and sent the ball in a high arc down the center. The good start buoyed her confidence.

"What did you say your last name was?" Grant strolled up next to her.

"Wendell."

"And you're a member here?"

She nodded. She didn't have to be a rocket scientist to see that he was pulling as much information from her as he could to figure out whom he was dealing with.

"Is your mother Trudy Wendell?"

Tamara almost stumbled. How had he made the connection so quickly?

"Yes."

"She's been hounding me at church to hold computer tutorial classes."

Tamara laughed loudly. "She tried to get me to do that, too. Maybe I should have used her to make my proposal."

"When I beat you and your new buddy, Norton, you can run home to your mother. You *will* need her to get me to do anything."

"Oh, so you're willing to play dirty mind games?"

They locked eyes for a moment before Grant turned away to take his shot.

Grant set up the next shot and hit the ball down the fairway. He didn't even bother to follow the arc with a gaze. Instead, he tapped in the divot with his heel, adjusted his clothing and put on his shades.

"Not bad. Let's see if Hadfield can match his boss's attempt." Tamara gave a finger wave and a bright smile. She waited for Hadfield to get into position, then sidled close to him. "Don't let Grant get inside your head," she whispered.

Hadfield stopped as the club was about to go on the upswing. His look of exasperation tickled her.

On the other hand, Grant glowered. She appreciated the expression since his frustration caused wonderful machinations with his mouth. Would his lips feel as soft as they looked to the touch of her fingers, or to the touch of her lips? She licked her lips as if she could sense the pressure of his mouth closing over hers.

Dang. The man had the power to make her hallucinate. She forced herself to snap out of it, and made her way over to the tee for her shot. She slowly and carefully set up her stance.

"Is this waiting game part of the plan?" Grant interrupted.

"It's called strategizing." She framed her gaze with her hand to shield her eyes. "You'll see why in a second." She wiggled her hips, keeping her feet apart and anchored. Her hands adjusted their grip around the club, opening and closing until she got it right.

Once her arms and club were in alignment, she moved to the next point. In a smooth, fluid motion, her upper body twisted like a tight coil. Her natural flexibility kicked in. When she reached the point of no return, she unwound with a constrained yet powerful motion. Her golf club followed through, connecting to the small white ball. The solid sound of the impact gave her a heads-up that she had scored a good hit—another one.

Holes three and four passed without any hitches. She'd gotten comfortable among the men, laughing at their jokes and exchanging a few of her own. This chance to meet and get to know the people who could mentor the teens couldn't have been more valuable. They were out of the corporate offices, away from the formalities that would affect any natural conversation.

Occasionally Tamara egged on Grant and Hadfield. But for the most part, she silently watched him interact with his junior team. His teaching method was patient and encouraged an unhurried approach to the problem.

It took almost an hour before the men loosened up enough around Grant to respond without sounding like robots. What she noticed and admired was the fact that they had started out as two separate teams, but now the junior managers were coaching each other.

Tamara stayed on the outside of the happy trio. Her growing admiration for the way Grant was coaching his employees went only so far. Her mission couldn't be compromised by her admiration—or by her traitorous body, which seemed to be overdosing on Grant's sexiness.

To get what she wanted, she had to win this game—nothing less.

Coming to the ninth hole, their scores were close. His continued goading irritated her like a scratchy sweater against her skin. His little annoyances and distractions were causing her to make silly mistakes. She was even more frustrated that she was allowing him to get under her skin.

But what he didn't know was that working under pressure excited her. And that more than anything, *he* excited her. She gave herself a pep talk.

She wiped away the sprinkle of sweat from her brow. Time to get down to business. She had work to do. Her eyes were on the prize, and the prize was time with Grant Benson. Ten young men waited for good news. She couldn't fail.

She tried to remember the golf tips she'd known in college. *Was it be one with the ball or with the swing?*

Out of the corner of her eye, she saw Grant's mouth moving. They'd both been filling each other's ears with trash talk, getting bolder as the hours wore on. She returned her focus to the ball, took a deep breath, drew back the club and exploded with a fast unwind that hit the ball low and straight. Her risky strategy should drop the ball a foot or so from the hole. Her plan was to make this a two-hitter into the hole.

Divine intervention had other plans, however. The ball soared, and with missile precision it hit the green and rolled into the hole. A hole in one.

Tamara couldn't believe it. She dropped her club and raised her hand in fierce victory.

Norton joined in with the noisy celebration. He whooped and jumped like a skittish colt in wide circles around his boss and colleague. They certainly weren't expressing sportsmanlike conduct. But this accomplishment was too sweet for a variety of reasons, and Tamara didn't care about etiquette. Her drive to win was as reckless as her plan to get face time with Grant had been.

Hadfield didn't look pleased, but he stayed as cool as his boss. Norton had now resorted to a few sloppy cartwheels. This time his teasing was solely at Hadfield's expense. Tamara guessed the two had a fairly competitive streak between them.

Grant, on the other hand, remained calm. Instead of the grimaces of frustration he'd had the whole game, he simply offered a golf clap or two. Then he approached the ball for his turn and swung. The ball shot straight ahead but then took a sharp veer to the right.

Game over.

"Mr. Benson, I'd say we've got a few matters to discuss," Tamara said with a smile.

"I think after beating me, you can call me Grant."

"And what do your friends call you?" Tamara asked, feeling bold.

"Are you proposing to be my friend?"

Tamara looked up at him, shielding her eyes from the sun.

"I'm just curious, that's all." She'd hold off on the friendship thing, for the moment.

"Let's see if we can cure that curiosity. I'm also Grant to my friends—new and old."

They headed back toward the clubhouse. Their pairing transitioned so that Tamara and Grant were walking together while Hadfield and Norton chatted amicably ahead of them. They walked side by side now, comparing notes about the latest goings-on in the community, the one common denominator between them.

"How come I don't see you around here?" Grant motioned toward the clubhouse.

"I have a place in the city. I don't like commuting."

"I recently bought a place here to get away from the ever-present paparazzi. My parents live with me."

"Oh, now that's a twist." Tamara waited for an explanation. The fact that he lived with his parents was a surprise. He was such a shadowy figure to pin down that picturing him hanging out with Mom and Dad in the family room didn't fit the image she had of him.

"They came kicking and screaming. I convinced them that the five-bedroom home was all theirs and that I'd move into the guesthouse on the premises."

"Okay, why on earth do you need such a place?" An over-the-top lifestyle didn't come to mind when she thought of Grant—not that she was ready to admit that he did dwell on her mind.

"This is a gift I'd promised myself I'd give them from the first day that my company opened. They've worked hard, sacrificed and never failed to show their love to my siblings and me. My mother loves to throw parties. She loves having her friends visit and stay. So, I gave her a house that is comfortable and inviting for her to enjoy. Plus it allows my father to disappear into one of the many rooms for his man cave."

"That's pretty cool."

"My siblings also pop in with their kids, and believe me, that noisy set can have that house hopping."

"One day that may be you. When you have a family of your own, you can have it bouncing."

No way that Grant couldn't easily find himself a bride. As he'd talked about his parents, he'd revealed how much of a family guy he was. However, she couldn't picture whom he'd pick as his soul mate. But soaking up his gorgeous features, she had no desire to fill in that mental image, anyway.

Tamara followed Grant to a table that overlooked the

course. Hadfield and Norton had disappeared toward the bigger clubhouse, which housed the fancier restaurants. She opted for the simpler fare.

The two restaurants in the smaller clubhouse catered to smaller groups and featured more of a deli menu. Since it was a weekday, the school-aged kids weren't around, and most of the retired crowd ate at the bigger restaurants, avoiding the sandwiches and deep-fried menu. The place was practically empty.

This venue was quieter, perfect. They could eat and get down to business. All she wanted was the time to deliver her request and get an immediate response. No candlelight suppers, no gourmet dining, no froufrou amenities as if this were a date.

They placed their order at the counter and then headed to the seating area.

Grant pulled out her chair. "Fat chance of me settling down," he said, resuming the conversation.

"Ever?"

"That's one thing I know for sure."

"Why? Because you're not the type to be taken home to a mother?" Tamara hadn't expected to get so personal, but she also hadn't expected him to be so forthright about his private life.

"Something like that. George Clooney is my role model. Eternal bachelor—live long and prosper, I say. Knock on wood." Grant knocked on the tabletop three times. "He and I are in the same fraternity."

Tamara had no issues with his viewpoint. After all, she also didn't want to be weighed down by any man— but it wasn't a women's liberation mind-set. She just figured that she could have the best of both worlds—like Oprah. Grant had his role model; she had hers.

No man had managed to make his way to the forefront of her thoughts. Right now, only her academy and the youth she helped had her focus. If a man came along who earned a place in her priorities, then he'd have to accept her dedication to her career. She still noticed male eye candy, but most times she didn't bother showing any signs of interest.

Sitting across from Grant brought that smooth medium brown complexion face-to-face with her. He certainly could own the label of eye candy. Even his hands, with long, slender fingers, drew her attention. His bared, muscled forearms flexed and relaxed as he motioned. The man turned the computer nerd stereotype on its head.

"I think our food is ready." She pushed back her chair to stand with him, but he raised his hands. "I've got it."

She nodded and accepted the kind gesture.

The more she talked to him, the less she wanted to see him just as eye candy. He had brains, and the fact that he had superhottie assets at the same time ratcheted up her approval ratings. The combination tickled her fancy, but she had no appetite for a little sample. What she wanted was to feast on his charisma, intelligence and physical strength. She knew she couldn't excite her palate for a bigger helping of sexy. Though her private body parts wanted in on the negotiations, she wasn't budging. Watching Grant and his succulent lips were as far as she was going with this fantasy.

"Chicken salad sandwich for you. I got the kettle chips because it was slim pickings."

"That's thoughtful." She waited until he was seated and had opened the wrapping for his sandwich before she began eating.

Tamara made small talk with Grant while they ate. She kept the topics away from her number one issue. Instead, they shared stories about living with aging parents. His parents honestly drew her interest; they sounded lively and fun-loving. Listening to his childhood antics with his siblings drew her laughter.

Eventually, they couldn't avoid the bigger issue.

Grant pushed aside his plate and leaned on his elbows. "I'm ready. Bring it on." He beckoned with his hand.

"All right, let's get down to business. I know you have other pressing engagements to attend to."

Grant nodded. The mischievous twinkle in his eye slid away to be replaced by a speculative gaze.

Grant prided himself on being organized and meticulous about his schedule. But his entire day up until this moment had had an off-kilter feel to it. As much as the unknown gave him indigestion, he had tried to go with the flow. That's what his sister always preached. He was too uptight. He needed to relax. Her last bit of advice wasn't appreciated when she'd said that the lack of a special someone in his life was messing with his chi. He hated when she got all metaphysical because she had a way of messing with his mind. As the youngest of three siblings, she didn't play by the rules, tricky little monster.

The day was past the halfway mark and the off-kilter feeling hadn't ended with the sexy presence of Tamara

Wendell in front of him. Because he had lost to her golf skills, he couldn't walk away and pretend that he was unmoved by her charisma.

"I'm listening," he prompted.

"As I've said, I'm the owner of New Horizons Leadership Academy, which works with the Miller-Brown Home for Boys. These are young men at critical junctions in life. Their run-ins with the law range from repeated trespasses after dark in city parks, to constantly fighting in school, to shoplifting at the local malls. They are faced with a future where communities are ready to lock them up and throw away the key. I eventually hope to expand my networks with other juvenile facilities, but for now, I've been working with them for the past two years."

"Noble. So, how are you funded?" Confusion deepened on Grant's face.

"Grants and private donations. I don't take a salary, therefore I can hire the best and the hardest-working people." A look of determination crossed her face. "We're a small team, but we're efficient and productive."

"And how do I fit in with all this? Yes, I run a company. I have a decent-sized staff. But, I have project deadlines to meet. You're asking me to take on a couple kids—"

"More like ten—"

"Ten! What the heck?" Grant waited for her to laugh and say that she was joking.

"Shh. Stop acting as if that's a problem. You can spread them around the company." Her defense came at him in a passionate wave.

Her intensity caused his eyebrow to pop up with surprise.

"Is this how you go about getting them jobs?" Those big brown eyes coaxed him just as hard as her soft, determined voice did. He found her presence to be dangerous to his resistance.

"Well, no. I've never had so many kids who couldn't be placed."

"What's wrong with them?" He frowned, waiting to hear some outrageous explanation.

"Nothing is wrong with them. They need a second chance." Tamara's chin raised a notch. Her entire body bristled under his question.

"Uh-oh, now you're killing me." Grant shook his head.

"Let me explain. These kids are difficult to place because of their juvenile records. However, the counselors and I believe that they are exceptional because their aptitude for learning is off the charts. And that's a good thing."

"But if they have antisocial behavior, you want me to risk my company and my employees with volatile kids who don't give a darn about anyone but themselves?" Grant pursed his lips. He hadn't meant to raise his voice.

"Don't paint them with a wide brush. You don't have a clue."

She might as well have poked him with a fiery pitchfork. His ears burned.

Grant pushed back. "Then if I'm so clueless, why are you coming to me?"

"I studied your company and you. You had passion, enough knowledge and some good luck to create Benson Technologies. People didn't always believe in you. Yet, you've become an icon in the industry."

"Don't pretend that you believe in me if you just want something from me." He didn't bother to hide the sarcasm. No matter how long someone talked to him, the person eventually showed his or her cards. Although she came at him with her own unique style, looking as fine as hell, she wasn't any different. Now he fought to pull back from her intense emotion before he tumbled down the hole into her crazy plan.

"I suppose everyone always wants a favor from you. You're a man with means. But I've been up front about what I want. This isn't about me. I'm fine. I'm comfortable. No, this is about stepping up to help others."

"You want me to help you so you can sleep at night?" He didn't let up, still smarting from her previous comment.

"You are impossible." Tamara stood. Her body bristled with fiery anger and indignation. Grant sensed that to be accused of being selfish cut her to the quick.

"I didn't expect that comment to be the one that would be the deal breaker. You were fighting with so much energy. Makes me wonder."

"Say one more word and I will empty this glass all over you."

"I wish your kids a lot of luck with such a hot-tempered advocate in their corner."

"You are being flip, and that's just plain irritating."

"Yes, I'm being deliberately annoying." He raised his glass in a salute. "But seriously, I don't make decisions of this magnitude just because a stubborn, albeit pretty, woman tries to shame me into surrender."

Grant noted how Tamara's mouth tightened and worked as if she was having a silent argument. He would love to know what she was fighting against to remain calm. This wasn't about her. Maybe she was one of those missionary wannabes who got a high off being the social worker because she basked under her ward's gratitude. Maybe playing the savior gave her a high.

After all, he didn't know her. She had done extensive homework on him, but he had been blindsided and played along. Now that she had put herself in his crosshairs, he meant to keep her there until he figured out the real deal. She couldn't be this kind, thoughtful and giving without expecting anything in return.

"I have a proposal with a bio about each boy in my car. At least look at them." She hesitated, waiting for his response.

Grant looked at his watch. "Let me walk you to your car. I do have to get back to work."

"Yes, of course."

Grant escorted Tamara to her car. He wished that he had the time to continue this discussion elsewhere. Her doggedness impressed him. Although deep down inside he knew that he would end up accepting her candidates, he wasn't quite ready to give in.

She unlocked her trunk and opened her briefcase. While she continued to extol the merits of each teenager, he flipped through the file.

They all exhibited academic excellence. But he'd have to lie if he said that their checkered pasts, and in some cases, too-recent run-ins with the law, didn't make his gut clench. On paper, they were extremes of good and bad.

Easy to see why most people would not give them a second look. As cold as it sounded, there were good kids who excelled just as well or better with nothing that was cringe-worthy in their backgrounds. Those were the ones being cherry-picked by the top companies, ready to be molded and tossed into the corporate culture of their sponsors.

But Benson Technologies had its own unique, indefinable culture. Grant prided himself on making sure that the environment didn't stifle creativity or create clones. But how far could he go with pushing the limits? Bringing on ten young men to be mentored was a job unto itself. As it was, he maintained a lean staff where everyone worked a job and a half.

"Please don't let my…actions and words stop you," Tamara said. "I'm laying it all on the table. Whatever you can do…" She handed him the last file. Her fingers tightened briefly as he took the file from her.

He touched her hand. "I promise not to let *you* sway my decision." Even as the words left his mouth, Grant had to cross his fingers on his other hand because he had already reneged on that promise.

Tamara had an eerie power of persuasion that was slowly affecting him. From the tantalizing scent of her perfume, to her sexiness, to her fearless stance, she influenced more than his mind. She caused his body to react as if it were under the influence of a potent drug.

From what she'd said, he surmised that she didn't have a plan B. He didn't think that he was too off the mark. Why else would she have spun herself into a low-grade twister, ready to take him out? Maybe time was running out to help these kids.

But how far did he want to go?

He tucked the files under his arm and walked away. He wasn't done with Tamara Wendell yet.

Chapter 4

A week had passed since Tamara Wendell had beaten him in a game of golf. Grant had taken the files she had given him back to his office, and now he'd finished reading each teen's bio. His decision to help hadn't wavered. How could it waver? He had once been one of those kids on the brink of heading down a bleak path.

Trespassing. Fighting. Truancy. He had earned his parents' displeasure and then some. It hadn't been until his father had landed a solid job and could get their family back together that Grant had turned a corner in his life. But those early years, consumed by poverty and despair, had ripped the family apart. He and his siblings had gone to live with a foster family while his parents had desperately tried to get their lives in order, determined to reunite the family.

Grant had taken on a rebellious attitude to steel himself against the shame and anger that had grown and swelled in his heart. By the time he was back with his parents, he was out of control. His father had quickly gotten tired of his bad behavior. Considering how hard his dad had been with him, Grant suspected that he hadn't been able to deal with feeling like a failure. Finally, a strong-willed mentor who didn't take any of his rage had gotten him on the straight path. But even now Grant hadn't stopped apologizing for putting his father through the wringer. The guilt still gnawed at his gut.

Now that Grant had information on the teens, he also wanted information on Tamara. He tossed the assignment to Deanna Rushgrove, his human resources manager, who handled background checks. If he did go along with Tamara's plan, he wanted to know, for purely business reasons, what type of woman he would be working closely with.

Come to think of it, Deanna had seemed a bit too eager to dig up any background details. Maybe the creative way Tamara had skirted his HR department to snag his attention had gotten under her skin. She'd even promised to have a file on his desk within the hour. He was looking forward to reading the good, bad and possibly ugly news about this interesting woman.

"Mr. Benson, the DBSK creators are here," said Latrice, his assistant, in a singsong voice.

"Show them in, please." Grant slid the files of the young men to the side of his desk. He had to get his mind back on his work. Nothing could get him to focus more than to dive into one of his works in progress.

As expected, two young men, no older than college

age, walked through the door. They had "born gamer" written all over them, despite the suits they wore.

"Have a seat, gentlemen. Jax, good to see you. Danny, have a seat." Grant stretched out his hand and noted their clammy hands. Understandably, their nerves were getting the better of them. He sat back in his chair, trying not to crowd them. People tended to forget that he was also a gamer at heart and only a businessman by necessity. But he didn't look at his business solely from a profit margin perspective.

"Mr. Benson, I…we…well, gosh, we are excited about the new venture." Danny Metcalf, the more exuberant of the two men, moved restlessly in his seat.

"So am I." Grant pulled out the mock-up of the game designs that had been completed so far. Normally the creators would meet with his design team, but this time he wanted to talk to the guys before anyone else got started on the brainstorm. What they had created promised to be epic.

Grant continued trying to make them comfortable. "Anything to drink—coffee, tea, soda?"

"I'll definitely take a soda." Danny raised his hand as if answering a question in a classroom.

"I'll join you with one. And you?" Grant noted that Jax Altman, the younger man, didn't say much of anything. Instead his pinpoint stare took in everything with a suspicious glint. Grant wondered if they were both on board with this deal. He wasn't about to invest his money and time only to be faced with partnership squabbles. His gut told him to continue onward, and this time he listened.

"Nothing."

Grant called Latrice for two sodas. He didn't wait for the beverages to get down to business. "I've been mulling over picking the right people for the team. I have two members of my staff who would be great to head up the project team. I'll introduce you to them later, but I want to talk a little bit about your vision."

"Why are you so interested in our vision? You're going to do what you want anyway." Jax crossed his arms and stroked his untrimmed beard.

"I have the right to do so, according to our contract. But I think we would work better if I have a keener sense of what you envision." Grant looked directly at Jax. "I don't want to start on a tumultuous note." He was used to working with the creative types and having to navigate both their emotions and their unique working styles. Running a gaming company had put him in a position where he'd had to hone those skills or risk having no staff.

Jax grunted. His expression gave away nothing.

However, Danny smiled brightly at Grant. "What would you like to talk about?"

"I understand the general gist of the game and its levels. But the overall objective…" Grant paused, trying to find the right words. The main premise was okay, but nothing that came out of his company should be only "okay." He wanted consumers to choose this game because there wasn't a substitute and because the experience was so unbelievably intense that they became addicted it. He wanted noteworthy. He wanted great. He wanted the characters to turn into cult classics.

He continued. "I see that on the surface, the computer game is about angels battling demons. But there're more nuances to the premise—in the world, not everything that seems to be perfect actually is perfect and not everything that appears to be evil actually is evil. In some cases, angels and demons switch sides with each other or transform back into humans."

"Exactly. Mythology is important. The users have to buy into the rules of the world or else nothing matters. Having interaction with the humans is going to be the big buzz. I think their roles can be ramped up." Danny didn't seem to take a breath during his response.

"I've been working on that." Now Jax sat forward. His posture always seemed as if he was poised to lift off. "Humans are agents to the angels or demons, but only certain ones can be turned."

"What's preventing all of them from being turned?" Grant looked at his notes. When world building, there couldn't be any holes. Other gamers lived to find faulty logic. Having a recall to fix a hardware issue or launching an upgrade to fix the design didn't fit with his standards for quality and delivery of the product. He'd never had to do that for any other project.

"That's not the goal of the angels or demons." Jax stroked his beard.

"Okay, but it doesn't explain why all humans aren't turned," Grant pushed. He popped his soda, already preparing for a long morning to iron out these important details.

"The goal is for one side to annihilate the other. The humans are caught in the middle of the battle. Their loss is collateral damage." Danny jumped in to explain.

Now that the conversation got under way, Danny

seemed to be in his comfort zone. Even Jax's suspicious attitude had softened.

"I think one of the levels should be a scenario where the humans could be used by one group," Grant suggested.

Jax nodded. "We can take a look at that."

This brainstorming process got his juices kicking. Grant sat back in the chair and sipped his soda. "We will do this." He raised his soda can and waited for Danny to follow suit, then they tapped the cans to their mutual success.

Now that his creative well had opened, he couldn't stop the flow of ideas. They remained in a huddle tossing around ideas, inventing, imagining and creating. Grant wrote copious amounts of notes to register the rules for this world. He scratched his temple, still thinking of additional possibilities.

More research on angel mythology from various cultures needed to be conducted to enrich the background. A vivid world paved the way for designers to create colorful, realistic scenes. Gamers were sophisticated end users who had to buy into the new world. They would form their expectations based on the intricate interweaving of the plot, their favorite characters and level of interaction with other gamers. Those components dictated if, at the end of the day, the gamers would spend the dollars to buy the new series.

After the men left to meet with Hadfield and Norton, Grant returned to his office. At his desk, he pushed up his sleeves, ready to sink his teeth into the work ahead. The power to create was intoxicating and made him feel as though he was floating high above the world, where he could admire its beauty. Most of his waking hours were consumed with his passion. His parents had gotten used to not seeing him for days, even though they lived on the property together. Meanwhile, he didn't give dating even a second thought. He couldn't split his time, his thoughts and his heart between his passion for games and a woman. It was out of the question.

Or so he repeatedly told himself whenever an aching loneliness did manage to sneak in and take hold. The increasing frequency of that loneliness was annoying. Lately, the feeling came whenever he thought of the stern face Tamara Wendell had made when she had been bending him to her will.

"Grant, here is the write-up on the Wendell woman." Deanna stood in the doorway of his office. He quickly beckoned her over to take a seat. She shook her head primly.

He reached for the file, noting how thin and light it felt in his hand. Exactly what did it contain? What would the contents reveal?

Deanna stood at his desk like a soldier at attention waiting for her next set of directives. His hand hovered over the file. He was eager to read over every detail about Tamara. She intrigued him with her brashness and her vigor for her work. Already feeling a bit of admiration, he'd rather keep his out-of-control emotions on the down low. He looked up at Deanna and reconsidered allowing her to stay. He respected her no-nonsense attitude with potential new hires. She could spot the weakness in someone's character, a skill that he found impressive and necessary to vet the ideal candidates. On the flip side, she was so eagle-eyed that the staff saw her as too cold and unapproachable. Tamara probably had had the misfortune to encounter this side of Deanna. Although later he would ask Deanna for her opinion, he wanted to savor any initial revelations without her input or her observation.

"Thank you, Deanna. I'll let you know if I need anything further."

"May I say something?" She pushed the thick black frames of her glasses up the bridge of her nose. Her frown covered her entire face, pinched and disapproving.

"In my professional opinion, I think that you need to be careful. There seemed to be discrepancies between—"

Grant raised his hand to interrupt. "It's okay. I will take all this in and decide." He wanted to add *on my own*.

Deanna left, plainly miffed at his dismissal. It wasn't the first time that he had gone in one direction when she had wanted him to go in another. Maybe one day his stubbornness would get the better of her and she'd quit. Hopefully that wouldn't be anytime soon, because she was good.

In the privacy of his office, with his schedule clear for the next hour, he took a deep breath. Anticipation built within, as if he was about to make a major discovery.

Slowly he opened the file, noting the scant paperwork. Only a few pages fluttered out of place. The first page was a neatly typed chart of personal information. Her middle name was Reggie. He sensed a story and wondered whom she was named after. She grew up in the public school system, a direct reaction to her parents' confidence in the merits of free education. She'd graduated with honors in childhood education, but then earned a master's in business marketing. Nothing else. He scanned the paper's contents once more. Her education wasn't a surprise. Yet, he wanted to connect the dots that had taken her from education to marketing to running an academy. Maybe the other paperwork would satisfy his growing list of questions. He suspected that there had to have been a catalyst for her desire to open an academy for at-risk young men. When had the pull to start the academy occurred? More important, what had caused that pull?

Tamara's face—confident, even a bit cocky, with dramatic features that made him look twice—was the outer cover of a fascinating and intriguing personality. Five minutes of talking to her had revealed how deeply she cared about the kids in her care. His instinct told him that she was for real.

He continued scanning the next page. She wasn't married. No children. No siblings. She had been interviewed only once, with her activist parents at an event facilitated by Oprah. Her family connections had certainly brought her close to various influential celebrities. As he looked at the chronology of events in her life, he surmised that maybe her father's terminal illness was a defining moment. The date of his death and the opening of the academy were close. The loss of such an important figure in her life must have been heart wrenching. From the way she talked about her mother, they had a close relationship. More than likely, they relied on each other to be strong. Honoring family held a high place in his philosophy of life, as well.

He read a newspaper clipping reporting on her father's passing. The close-knit family had had to deal with his early death in a public way because he had been a prominent figure. Her father's lengthy illness had caused him to have to cancel many events. As a result, Tamara and her mother had stepped up and filled many of the appointments. Supporters praised her direction, although she drew criticism for not being as powerful as her father. According to the article, she didn't have the oratory power of her father, but Grant didn't agree. She had had the power to sway him with her magnetic charisma.

A few snide articles called her the trust fund activist. There was a sole picture of her exiting a nightclub with friends, which had earned the wrath of a writer who was eager to vent about today's youth. He was about to turn the page when he noticed that Tamara had issued a letter to the editor, taking the writer to task for being narrow-minded and not performing the proper research. He admired her for defending herself. That spark of fire that he had seen flash in her eyes when she was making a point had stirred up more than his approval. It was closer to an arousal.

But he had the desire to go deeper than these reports. The bare-bones information didn't feed every detail of his curiosity. He was intrigued, and admittedly suspicious, that she chose this vocation when her life could have been lived with relative ease. Yet, if she was so down-to-earth with her students, why did she hobnob at the country club wearing designer fashion from head to toe and drive a shiny Bentley?

He suspected there were two sides to Tamara. He wondered which one was real. His schedule was filled for days, but he planned to make revealing the real Tamara Wendell a new priority. If there was one iota of questionable behavior from her or her students, he would be done with her. She'd regret the day that she had brazenly crashed his golf game.

One way to get close to her would be to accept her proposal to place the at-risk guys in his company. But he didn't want to use the teens like that. He'd do his best for them, even if his charitable nature didn't extend to their mentor.

Yes, he would enjoy uncovering Tamara. His thoughts drifted to the actual act of uncovering, disrobing, the full reveal. The thought of those hips that she'd wiggled at him at each hole sent him into a tailspin of dirty thoughts. At least nine times, not that he had counted, she had caused him to have to bite his inner cheek to remain cool while his sexual energy had been beating in his body.

Chapter 5

Latrice knocked and popped her head into his office. Before she could utter a word, Vanessa Lord sidestepped his assistant to gain entry.

"Hello, Grant. It's so good to see you."

Grant roused himself from his wandering thoughts and focused on the woman in front of him. He had been expecting her. She had invited him to lunch, but he'd turned that down and instead had invited her to his office. He wanted no misperception on her part that this meeting was a date.

He waved away Latrice before turning his attention on his ex-fiancée. "Let's have a seat over here." He motioned toward the suite of furniture arranged for small meetings.

"You know, I was worried that you weren't going to meet me." Vanessa's tone took on a whine. No matter how unattractively she acted, she had the good fortune to look like a model: perfect face, perfect body and perfect fashion sense. He had known her long enough to know that the perfection didn't go much farther than the outer shell. She had a mean, selfish streak that ran deep and hot like the earth's magma center.

"You said that you had something important to say that had to be said in person," Grant began. "I know you had a health scare recently. So I dropped what I was doing to meet with you. And that's the only reason why you're here."

He'd dated Vanessa for a year. Even now he was ashamed to say that he had been infatuated with her beauty. Having a supermodel be interested in him and pursue him had played with his ego. Truly, if he'd bothered to pay attention to his instincts, and especially his mother's nagging, he would have avoided the major damage Vanessa had caused.

They had had nothing in common. She'd wanted to take the relationship to the next level, so he'd given in and proposed. But he had listened to his father and brought up a prenup agreement. Grant still hadn't recovered from the ringing sound of her enraged shriek when he'd mentioned the word *prenup*. Their breakup had resembled a violent tornado, and Vanessa had unleashed her venom until the law had had to intervene. Now he didn't have a problem closing off his heart to her. But when he'd heard that she had battled breast cancer, he'd allowed a thaw in their relations. But since their painful and bitter breakup, he'd had no appetite to connect more than casually with any woman, much less ask anyone on a date.

Vanessa flipped her hair over her shoulder. "My mother wants to meet you again."

He was certain that she knew how much he'd once admired the length and grace of her neck that now showcased her thick, luxurious hair cascading over one shoulder. The difference today was that she meant nothing to him; therefore, nothing she did registered even a blip on his radar.

"Your mother? Meet me? Again?" An icy trickle of fear slithered down his spine. He twitched involuntarily. "Are you pregnant?" He hadn't been with her in over a year, but that never stopped someone from tossing out the accusation. He pushed on, not even waiting for an answer. "Is it about your health?"

She waved her hand in a dismissive gesture. "I'm fine. No baby." She tapped her flat stomach and then pulled out a cigarette. "I'd have to put these down, and nine months without one isn't going to happen." She shifted her expression into more of an amicable, easygoing countenance. "I admitted to my mom the other day how much I was moved by your thoughtful gift when I was sick. Gosh, and those flowers were to die for. Can you believe some people didn't even send me a get-well email?" Her brow knitted, as if the reason for the snub was beyond her comprehension. "Ever since then, you've been on my mind. I think that I've fallen in love with you all over again."

"And you told this to your mom?" Suddenly Grant needed a drink of water. "I don't think this conversation is for me."

"It's more than just talk. You're my soul mate. I know because when you close your eyes, you should be able to hear your soul mate's voice or see his face instantaneously."

Grant wanted to object. He knew that closing his eyes conjured only Tamara's face. And, as a point of fact, there was no way that he thought of Tamara as his soul mate. Even she would issue one of her throaty, guttural laughs at that notion.

"This conversation is over." Grant pushed back from his chair and stood. "I don't know what you'd hoped would happen. Frankly that doesn't matter." He signaled in the space between her and him. "*We* are over."

"I was hoping that you'd change your mind." Vanessa's smile wavered. "If you meet with my mother, she'll make you understand—"

"Stop. I shouldn't have done this." He didn't want to give life to something that was long dead and buried. He hated being the bad guy and feeling as if he was being insensitive, but truly nothing lingered in his heart for her. And he didn't want any reminders of what could have been with Vanessa as his wife.

"I don't mind signing the prenup. I even brought a copy." She smoothed out a copy of the original document. "I shouldn't have listened to my girlfriends. They said that you weren't in love with me if you had to give me a prenup." She wiped the tears from her eyes. "All I'm asking for is a second chance." She wiped another escaping tear.

The more that Vanessa reiterated her point, the more Grant withdrew. No part of him wanted anything to do with Vanessa. He had made the mistake of settling for her, letting his ego get the better of him, rushing toward a fantasy that had remained elusive.

When he thought of beauty, brains and a sexy body that could cause a fantasy or two, only one person came to mind—Tamara Wendell. But he was wiser and much tougher now, and he knew that there was no real connection with Tamara. How could there be? The sexual nudge to his system when he was around her or even thought about her was only a tiny spark. He didn't want to call it anything more significant.

"Let's end this conversation on a civil note, shall we? Good-bye. And I wish you well, Vanessa."

More tears welled in Vanessa's eyes. Underneath the sorrow, he could see the anger of being scorned. The niggling sense that this might not be over hung in the room. He knew that she could go from sorrow to rage in an instant. A relationship that had started as a blind date had now turned into a recurring nightmare.

Vanessa gathered up her purse. "Since you are a man who hasn't given up on his dream, then you should recognize a kindred spirit. I won't give up on mine." She stood with an erect posture, turned and walked away from him with her head held high. In a final show of anger, she flung open the office door and marched past a bewildered Latrice, who had to scoot back to get out of Vanessa's way.

Grant didn't move. He wasn't worried about Vanessa's new obsession, at least not in a way that made him worry about his safety. Instead, he wondered how much of a bother she'd be, especially once he notified security that she was persona non grata. *Her mother! Like hell that would happen.* He shook his head at the thought.

Grant wasted no time in calling Latrice and passing on his new instructions about Vanessa. Now that he'd wasted an hour, he had to get back to work. On his list of things to do was to call Tamara with his decision.

By the time he'd wrapped up pending items on his desk, he had changed his mind about calling Tamara. "Latrice, get in touch with Tamara Wendell. Let her know that I'm on my way to her academy to talk to her."

Paying a visit to Tamara wasn't on his to-do list, but dealing with Vanessa had royally screwed his mind from concentrating on anything. Tamara's face had been popping into his head all day, and he wanted to see her. Plus, what better way to observe her than on her turf?

Grant left Rockville and headed over to the academy on the other side of the Beltway that wound around Maryland, Virginia and Washington, D.C. The academy was nestled on the outskirts of College Park, near the main campus of the University of Maryland. The mainly residential area had been split into several subdivisions along the Baltimore and Ohio Railroad.

As he crested a steep hill in his car, New Horizons Leadership Academy popped into view. The red brick building had been a middle school. Its former name was still etched in the bricks arched over the entrance. The area looked worn around the edges. There were a few homes nearby that had For Sale signs or whose doors and windows were boarded shut. A dog ambled down the road, barking halfheartedly at his car. He pulled into the parking lot, surveying the area for any signs of life. A few cars were already parked. Otherwise, there weren't signs of anyone.

The grass around the school had been recently mowed, and there was a small flower garden outlining the property. A fenced-in play area with new playground equipment was situated off to the side. Despite the dreary neighborhood and dated style of the school, a fresh coat of paint had been applied to the trimmings and windows. He was impressed with the efforts made to enhance the community.

He walked up the few steps leading to the massive entrance door. The door was locked, and not until he announced his name through the intercom was he allowed entry. Stepping into the lobby, he could see the signs of a small community of children. He stepped beyond another door and a glass wall and noticed that the classrooms were occupied. One class of young children was singing, another one was writing and another was listening to the instructor read from an oversized picture book.

Nowhere did he see any older teens. Considering it was only two o'clock, they may still be in school. He looked forward to learning more about them and their time at the academy. He wanted to do his own research so that he could make an independent decision. But his first impression was crucial. He walked back to the lobby and was greeted by the receptionist.

"May I help you?"

"I'm here to see Tamara Wendell."

"Grant, good to see you."

That familiar husky voice greeted him from behind with a crisp, businesslike tone. His shoulders instantly tensed…waiting. He turned to face her. She had approached from the hallway and was now stopped with arms crossed and a hip cocked to the side. He was ready for her signature brashness and cocky smile.

Instead, she pinned him with a cool look. Yes, she

smiled. Yes, she welcomed him. Those eyes, however, fastened on him and cast a cool, disdainful inspection over him. What had he done?

"Come this way." She led the way to the first room and stepped aside in the doorway to her office. More than a little curious, Grant approached her, almost ready to tiptoe across the room if that would relax the tension. He imagined how any misbehaving student must feel to be summoned by her. Yet, she appeared more irritated than angry about his presence. He followed her invitation.

As Grant walked into her office, he readied himself for her attack. Surely, there had to be a reason for the icy reception. One thing for sure, he had no intention of leaving until he found out why she seemed prickly. He paused, wanting to confront her for an explanation. Her perfumed scent tantalized his senses, causing wild thoughts to form. What if he reached out to lift her small chin? What if he smoothed back the wayward strands of her hair? What if he kissed her mouth and tasted those full lips that toyed with his imagination? He struggled to get his breathing under control.

Mere feet away from her now, he noted all the small details of where her moles dotted her skin, the various shades of auburn that streaked throughout her hair and the natural lift of her round eyes, which added to their unique beauty. Under different circumstances, he would be tempted to touch her silky hair and let his fingers gently comb it into submission.

However, he risked his fingers being broken and handed back to him if he tried that move now. Taking the safer route, he muted his explosive, internal reactions and looked around at her office.

"Wow!" Grant exclaimed. "This is an awesome setup you have." He spun around in a circle to admire the room.

The decor was neither haphazard nor average as many offices were. Instead, the room infused him with a sense of calm, mixed with easy comfort. She had created an inviting place away from the hectic world beyond her office walls. He didn't know the specifics of the color spectrum, but he knew what he liked. And the various shades of soft browns mixed with the bolder richness of gold hues created a soothing mood in the room.

She didn't use the average, heavy office furniture. Clean and efficient could describe the modern flair of the desk, bookcases and chairs. The bookcases were filled with a variety of books and magazines geared toward younger readers.

"I have an open-door policy with my students and staff. They can come in and read or talk or take a calming time-out."

"And you work in here?"

"For the most part. I have a smaller room if I need privacy. But I never want to shut myself off at the academy."

"I see you also have a day care."

"Yes, there is always a need for a good day care. It's fairly new to our list of activities. We provide the day care throughout the day, and then our after-school program is for the older teens."

"You've done a lot in over a year. I read up on the

academy and was surprised that you have seventy-five boys and that they're all between the ages of twelve and eighteen. Some of the boys who have moved on spoke highly of you and the staff in their testimonials."

She sighed, and her shoulders relaxed. "Have a seat, please." Her wary gaze still hovered over him.

He complied. This quieter version of Tamara made him uneasy. He had gotten used to her exuberance by the end of their game last time. How could he not admire her tenacity and energy? Even Hadfield and Norton still reminisced about the game, dropping heavy hints that they wanted to play again with her.

From the cool reception she'd given him, he doubted that she'd volunteer to fill in for a game of golf.

"How can I help you? Your assistant's insistence that I see you today has made me curious."

"I wanted to talk some more about your proposal."

"I didn't think you were interested. It's been a week." A slight tone of disapproval crept into her tone.

"I've been thinking about it every day," he countered. He couldn't stop thinking about her grand plan, but mostly he couldn't stop thinking about her.

She crossed her arms, clearly waiting for him to continue. Her chin jutted out, ready to take him to task for any perceived slight. Now she made him tense.

The distance between them seemed like hundreds of feet, and a thick layer of frost covered the gap.

"So you want my company to commit to six months with ten guys." Grant repeated the proposal to ensure that they were still on the same page.

"Yes." Now her foot tapped. If he waited any longer, he expected to see her explode from the anticipation.

"I want to talk about the young men." He wasn't ready to give in just yet.

"What would you like to know?"

"I don't want more information about them. I want to talk to them—that's what my assistant should have told you."

"She did. However, your request is a bit unusual. No one has ever asked to meet them before taking them on."

"I play by my own rules."

"Nothing wrong with that. We're kindred spirits in that regard."

The term *soul mate* lingered in his thoughts.

"And I never said that I wasn't taking them on."

"But you didn't say that you would," she accused.

She blinked rapidly, staring straight ahead.

"Then for the record, Benson Technologies will extend an internship offer to ten students whom you've preselected. We can begin next Monday."

"Thank you." She was already on her feet, and she picked up the phone. "Mitzy, hold a sec." She covered the mouthpiece. "Do you have time to return tomorrow afternoon? They will be here."

He nodded without checking his schedule. Short of an emergency, nothing else mattered at the moment.

She returned her attention to the phone. "Mitzy, could you arrange for that list of students to come to the academy tomorrow?" After instructing Mitzy about other tasks, Tamara hung up. "I hope that this doesn't interfere with your schedule too much."

"I'll make the time."

She nodded, pleased with his response.

The mood lightened considerably. Now Grant felt

more relaxed, as if he'd been given a reprieve from the formidable academy owner.

She clapped her hands and issued a fat grin at him.

"I knew that I could count on you." She pointed at him, and with a squinty gleam continued, "You are the perfect match for these kids. You had me worried a little, though, when I didn't hear from you. I couldn't understand how you would not want to help these guys."

"I'm glad that I can set your mind at ease. But I do have a request. Consider it an exchange for doing business. You may want to sit." Grant waited for her to resume her seat opposite him at her desk. What he was about to propose might knock her off her feet.

Tamara took her seat. Her nerves had been rattled from the moment he'd walked into her office. If he only knew how she was one step from melting every time he stood close to her. Grant Benson's charisma and sexiness made her heart race and took care of pushing her cardio endurance to the limit.

First, he had delivered his acceptance of her proposal with enough drama to make her eye twitch. Now, he was tossing out a request with a sexy mysterious abandon that warned her not to expect the ordinary.

Becky had referred to the sexy meter. From head to toe, Grant was an image of a man who was anything but the computer nerd stereotype. The man could easily grace any runway or magazine cover sporting designer high-end clothing to cool casual wear. He had been blessed with the right package—a lean muscled figure with wide shoulders, tapering down to slim hips and long legs—and an indefinable aura of physical presence. The sizzling-hot, walking sex trap had the power to ensnare unsuspecting females if they got too close. And yet, she wanted to reach out, to get close, to touch the danger. Her body craved that touch. In the confines of the office, she got hot just thinking about having his hands on her body and straddling him. She said a quick prayer for restraint. Her body quivered as his dark gaze swept over her. She adjusted her position in the chair, hoping that any movement on her part could snap the hypnotic pull he seemed to have over her.

"I have a proposition," he repeated, after clearing his throat.

Tamara remained silent. She wanted to do more than clear her throat. She needed a cold glass of water to put out the flames of desire that burned out of control.

"Since I have been able to help you, I would like to ask something of you in return."

"This is a charitable institution. I can't imagine how I could repay you." She readied herself for whatever ridiculous demand he would concoct.

"I want a rematch."

"A what?"

"I don't like losing. I want a rematch," he repeated.

Tamara had to admit that she hadn't seen that one coming. "You don't like losing, or you don't like losing to a woman?"

"Only losing in general. The fact that you're a woman doesn't turn me off."

Tamara's heart felt as if it had done a double pump. Plus, had his gaze just slid down from her face to rest a few seconds on her breasts? Thank goodness she'd worn a blazer over her silk blouse. Her nipples were tight and on point.

"I'm sure that I can squeeze in a golf game—" she replied.

"No, no. I want to choose the game." He leaned forward, planting his elbows on his thighs. His hands and long slender fingers hung over his knees with annoying casualness.

"What game?" Her voice rose a bit.

He paused. "Haven't decided. I just needed to know that you'd honor the challenge."

"You're sneaky."

"Not sneaky at all. I simply want a do-over. I feel as if you had the advantage over me from the beginning."

"And now you're going to turn the tables?"

"No. Just make things even from the start." He smiled, but she swore that there was more devilishness than innocence in the smile. It intrigued her.

"And is that it?" she asked.

"No." His smile transformed to a full grin.

She noted the small dimple that surfaced between the corner of his mouth and cheek. Her thumb itched to caress it.

He continued. "I have one more request."

"No wonder you're at the top of your industry. You're in the 'one for you, two for me' mind-set. Let me remind you, again, that we are a charitable institution."

"I seize opportunities as they're presented. But I don't mow down my competitors. I don't eliminate my enemies. And I don't abuse my friends." He leaned back in his chair. "I just see this as an opportunity to get to know you. With what I can offer your students, I can't imagine you'd turn me down."

Had he just threatened her? Tamara remained silent, but her defenses had already started mounting.

"And because of that, really, I want to take you on a date."

"Date?" She could muster only the one word because her brain was a jumble of words too incoherent for a full sentence.

"I could have lied and called it a business meeting. But I'd rather lay things out on the table."

Tamara needed a drink immediately. She popped up out of the chair and got a water from the mini refrigerator near her desk. She filled her mouth with water until her cheeks puffed out like a squirrel hoarding nuts. The reprieve from sitting across from Grant and dodging his scrutiny did her some good. This was one intense conversation, and she could use a few interruptions to collect her thoughts.

Grant hadn't moved since she'd gotten the water. She stared at the back of his neatly trimmed head, still bewildered by his desire to go on a date. All along, she'd figured that her attraction was one-sided. And was it even a good idea to go on a date with someone she'd be working with?

Chapter 6

"Mr. Benson, I think that a date is too personal." Tamara resumed her seat. "I can't go on a date with you." She took a long drink from the water bottle.

Grant sucked in his breath. "Ack. You've gone formal on me. Please, no need to draw the battle lines. I'm still Grant." He took a deep breath. "Here's my solution. You call it a business meeting. I'll call it a date. By the way, I expect that we'll have many of those meetings to talk about the progress of your students. I'm personally going to oversee their internship."

"Thank you for that. However, a date is unnecessary. I don't operate my business in that manner."

"Very noble. But, I want to understand the woman behind all of this."

"I'm sure you're a busy man. So, right here, right now, you can ask me your questions and be done." Tamara wanted to reach out and strangle Grant. If he only had any idea how much she wanted to be on a date with him and how difficult it was to put her professional integrity before her desire.

"True, I am always busy. Since I'm stretching my staff and resources to accommodate your army of teens, I think I should be allowed this small measure of appreciation."

Had he just flashed that darn dimple at her again? She had to give him his props. This in-person invasion had all been carefully calculated, and he was doing a good job of portraying her as paranoid and ungrateful if she didn't take him up on the date.

"How many women have you coerced into going on dates with you?" Tamara didn't really expect an honest answer.

"Now, that's an insult if I've ever heard one. I hope you don't think I'm forcing you in any manner."

She knew that she could have asked the question with more finesse. However, she wasn't withdrawing the question or apologizing for it.

"I'm curious about you. Aren't you curious about me?" he asked.

"You think a lot of yourself," she replied.

"If I don't, who will? You are being very difficult on a simple matter."

Tamara made her decision. "Okay, but no strings attached."

"I've heard that before."

"Excuse me?" She frowned at the unexpected bitter edge to his remark.

"Sorry. I wasn't inferring anything about you."

"So you want a rematch and a date?" Tamara stood so she'd be able to look down on him. Grant wasn't going to be in the driver's seat on this arrangement.

He also stood, his height towering over her. He casually posed with his hand in his pants pocket, looking relaxed. What was going through his mind right now?

"Why are you looking so intense?" he asked with a maddening smirk.

"Trying to figure out what fate is trying to tell me now that I've met a rich bachelor who's demanding, greedy and self-absorbed."

"You missed the mark on a few of those descriptors, though." He offered a cheesy grin.

"What? I think that I've managed to sum you up." Tamara didn't like that she couldn't control her own chaotic feelings while he maintained a casual, playful demeanor.

"I'm compelling, dedicated and not hard on the eyes."

"All of that would matter if I was engaging you for more than this meeting," Tamara remarked. She could survive one date with him. No guarantees what condition she'd be in after, but she wasn't going to let him turn her world upside down.

"Are you interested in more than one business meeting?"

"No!"

She suspected that he was toying with her. While he may get satisfaction from this little stunt, she refused to play any part of his game.

"Now, that was said with a lot of passion. Who broke your heart?"

"Don't have one to break." Tamara bit her lip, wishing that she could retract her outburst.

"No heart?" He looked puzzled.

"I don't have a *romantic* heart. And you and your kind that try to fool women with a lot of dazzle and bling can take your gimmick elsewhere."

"Apologies for the morons of my gender." He stepped into her space with a bold forward stride. She instinctively took a step back. "But you intrigue me." His head tilted to the side.

"The feeling is not mutual." She fidgeted under the scrutiny. The way he looked at her reduced her to feeling transparent.

"Liar." His accusation came with a chuckle.

"You're a piece of work."

"That's what my little sister says to me when she's irritated. I'll take it as a term of endearment."

"Is this how you operate? Flirting with all your business associates?"

"I'm not a player, not by any stretch of the imagination." He looked down at his clasped hands. "I only came over to say that I will mentor your students. Standing in this room with all its personality made me wonder about the person behind this vision. And I'm in awe of all that you've accomplished."

"You're making this professional relationship more difficult."

"I don't mean to do so." He reached above her head and pulled back the vertical blinds. "I tend to speak my mind. Right now on my mind is the memory of the first time that I met you in the clubhouse lobby. There was a wide tract of sunlight that cut across the floor. You stepped into that light and it framed you like a spotlight on stage. You were like a bold brew of dark coffee in the morning—nothing better for the system."

"Mr. Benson...Grant, now, that's a first for me. I've never been compared to a morning beverage."

"Let's just give our business meeting the green light to go ahead."

She nodded with a quick bob of her head.

His only response was to keep his hooded gaze lingering on her mouth.

If she had any spunk, she'd tiptoe closer and put an end to wondering what it would be like to kiss him. Unfortunately, her feet were too firmly planted for such nonsense.

"I will be on my way now." He stepped away from her. "Pick you up at seven. I'll need your info."

"Seven?"

"Yep. Tonight. Is that a problem?"

Tamara wrote her address, which was difficult since her mind was still in shock over how quickly this was all happening. She'd be lying if she didn't admit that his direct style turned her on.

"See you later, then." He exited the room, leaving her standing in place, staring at the space where he'd just been.

Tamara nodded to the empty room. She couldn't seem to outthink this man and respond to his unusual questions at the same time.

Leave it up to the successful business owner to step boldly into her office with his brazen proposals. Maybe he wasn't used to hearing no or having someone push back. So far, she had proved that she wasn't the type to push back. Well, she'd play along, but it was clear she had absolutely no intention of falling for the easy compliments that had slid from his lips.

Fantasizing about dating him and actually going on a date with him were two very different things. Both stirred up her emotions like a craving for the sweetest piece of fruit.

Mitzy popped her head into the office. "Tamara, I confirmed with Miller-Brown that those students will be here tomorrow after school."

"Good. Let Grant know the details."

"Who?"

"Mr. Benson. Please let him know." Tamara took a pass on calling him herself. No matter how brief, she needed a break from Grant to resettle her thoughts. There was still work to be completed today. Now that her mind was in a muddled state, she'd have to work harder to concentrate. Thoughts about what she'd wear that night were already vying for her attention.

Tamara fought against daydreaming at her desk. Thank goodness for the little children whose fun energy filled the hallways. Before too long, she was huddled next to them, listening to their opinions about their day. A few parents arrived early to pick up their children, and she took the time to chat with them. Their feedback always helped to enhance what she could offer to them. They didn't have the resources for a large number of children, but the limited size allowed her staff to give more attention to the children and to the finer details of child care.

Watching the clock became an addiction for her. As

the afternoon crept to a close, Tamara assisted the day-care leaders with cleaning their classrooms. Activity would pick up again in the next half hour. The after-school youth were due to arrive in waves once the day-care children were picked up. She never left the building at that time if she could help it.

Her lean staff of five had specific tasks, but they didn't have a problem with rolling up their sleeves to help one another. Their strong team ethic had kept their operation running smoothly. Their loyalty meant everything to her.

At five-thirty, she finally felt comfortable enough to leave. Grant would have to wait if she were late. Playing at date night with him was not more important than her duties at the academy. Anyway, she had already texted Becky, who had had meetings outside the academy that day, to meet her at home.

She gathered up her briefcase with pending files and headed for her car. Work didn't stop at any particular hour for her. When she came back from her meeting with Grant, she had to get the details of Becky's meetings. Her friend was meeting with local government officials for their support. All the political maneuvering mattered when donations and grants were largely depended upon to keep the doors open.

Tamara thanked all the green traffic lights that got her to her parking garage in record time. She dropped her briefcase in the living room and ran toward her bedroom, pulling off pieces of clothing and tossing them aside. Her forward momentum didn't stop until she stood under the forceful spray of her showerhead.

Tamara looked at the array of shower gels in the

basket caddy. She could smell like cocoa butter, have soft skin from the shea butter, or avoid dry skin with the heavy cream moisturizer. What difference would it make? His hands wouldn't be touching her skin. She grabbed the original, unscented shower gel bottle. No need to tempt fate.

"Hey, Tamara!" A round of knocking interrupted Tamara's musing. Becky had obviously arrived home.

"What?" Tamara called. She turned off the shower.

"Hurry up. We've got to figure out your clothes, hair, makeup. You know it'll take hours to get you together. And you don't have that kind of time."

"Thanks for that." Tamara toweled off and put on her underwear and bra. Her nerves started their hum. Her stomach clenched. The reality that she'd be with Grant in less than an hour made her want to dash back into the shower and run the cold water this time.

She emerged from the bathroom to see Becky grinning as if she'd won a shopping spree at her favorite shoe store. Her hazel-green eyes practically sparkled with happiness on Tamara's behalf. When Tamara had texted Becky the news, her friend had called back to unload an ear-deafening scream.

"I wish you'd stop acting so weird," Tamara complained.

"Why? Because my faith has been restored? I was thinking that you needed major intervention to step out there and have a romantic fling."

"Romance isn't for everyone, Miss Bleeding Heart Romantic Fanatic."

"I think you just cursed at me. Whatever! I can't help believing in love."

Becky would always be the bright light in the stormy waters of falling in love. No matter how many times she got her heart broken, she got right up on that horse and rode toward the windmills with her happy thoughts. That was a trip that Tamara didn't plan to take, unless it was on her terms. There would be no *falling* in love. Tamara would very carefully *walk* down that path without the head trip that some women went through.

Becky now lay across her bed, her head propped up on her hand. "Could you move any slower?" Her impatience settled over the room.

Tamara waved off Becky's irritation. "Stop giving me the evil eye. At least I am out of the bathroom."

"Took you long enough. You were acting as if you hadn't showered in months." Becky sat up. Now her irritation gave way to excitement again. "So where are you going?"

Tamara shrugged. "I was too in shock to remember to ask such questions."

"Then how can we decide if the outfit should be formal, evening-elegant, casual or torn-jean attire?"

Tamara shook her head. "I told him that this was a business meeting."

"Yeah, you said that to me, and I don't get that. Stop playing hard to get. What's his only crime? That he's rich?"

"I don't have a problem with his wealth." Tamara was okay with the small lie.

"Please, I know how you think. You're in your Caped Crusader mode, off to save the masses." Becky wrapped the bedsheet around her shoulders and struck a fierce pose. "He is the powerful tycoon who has done wrong just by enjoying his wealth and success. The poor man won't stand a chance with your crazy mind-set."

"That's nonsense." Tamara hated when Becky could pick her apart. "Anyway, spare him the sympathy card. You should have heard him earlier today."

"Heard what you thought he said? Or heard what he actually said? One day, I'll be so lucky to meet some-one like him." Becky closed her eyes. A dreamy smile wavered on her mouth.

If anyone deserved happiness and a good man, it was Becky. She was a sweet soul, with so much patience and trust that men took advantage of her kindness. Between her and Becky, they hadn't had too many successful relationships. And yet, Becky wasn't afraid to dip her toe, her leg, her entire being into that romantic pool of love. Well, one of them needed to stay on the shore to pull the other to safety.

Tamara was up for the role of lifeguard. When she found a mate worthy of her standards, she still didn't plan to demand marriage vows that would be broken upon the least temptation. She was going in with eyes wide open and the panic button ready to be pushed, just in case.

"I want to go with casual business," Tamara declared.

"Boring."

"That's the idea," Tamara replied.

"You know, I'm beginning to think that it's not that you're playing hard to get."

Tamara headed to her closet. Becky was about to go on a psychoanalytical rant.

"You don't want to be swayed by this man. You can play indifferent with someone else, but I've noticed how you light up when we talk about him." Becky walked to the side of her bed and retrieved a hardcover book. "And you read this biography on him as if you were studying for a test."

Tamara ran her hand over her blouses. She pretended to study one then another. Protesting would only confirm Becky's observations. She pulled out a beige top.

"Oh, no, not that one. You look like a missionary ready to perform some conversions. And in this case, we need him to convert to you. He'll have his work cut out for him. Those clothes that you're planning to wear would make a man snooze."

Tamara shook her head at her friend's silliness.

"That's how I keep out of trouble. You, on the other hand, have attracted nothing but trouble with your crazy get-ups. And when things get out of hand, I get blamed."

Their last year in high school came to mind. Becky had thought it was a good idea to go on the hunt for a prom date at her older brother's college campus. Not only did they get caught for skipping school, but they got in a lot of hot water for pretending they were older. Becky usually instigated, but Tamara was gullible enough to take on the challenge. They'd get caught, and immediately everyone thought that Tamara was solely at fault.

"And you've earned my best-friend-forever status." Becky giggled.

"You're so kind." Tamara could never stay mad at her friend. They were soul sisters, through thick and thin.

"Now, how about this outfit?" Becky had joined her in the closet to select clothes.

"That pair of pants doesn't work. A bit on the tight

side." Tamara patted her hips. A few inches always managed to play hide-and-seek around her hips, making her curvier than she'd prefer.

"Nothing wrong with skintight. Wear a long blouse, if that'll make you comfortable."

"I'm not trying to hold my breath for the entire evening." As it was, she'd be having all kinds of breathing issues whenever she came into close proximity to Grant. Worrying about popping the button from her pants in front of a hunky man was an experience that she'd rather avoid.

"Pull out that pair of black jeans. Now grab that electric blue top."

"What if it gets cold?" Tamara eyed the lightweight fabric and low-scooped neckline.

"Then wear this black blazer. You'll look all slim and trim in the black. And the blue will light up your face."

Tamara slipped on the clothes. She had to admit that Becky's picks did work.

Becky pointed to her feet. "Shoes?"

"Flats."

"Boring."

"This is business."

"You sound like a broken record. Anyway, who is in control?" Becky was on her knees, pulling out shoes for closer inspection.

"Sometimes, I'm not sure." Tamara sighed.

"Then take control of one thing—his sexual appetite. I'll be right back." Becky left the room but hurried back with her latest shoe purchase.

"You want me to control Grant's sexual appetite with your three-and-a-half-inch stilettos?"

"Yeah, baby. These heels will make your hips do that slinky, sexy walk."

Tamara didn't doubt the claim. She slipped her feet into the shoes. Immediately her calves tightened and she had to readjust her body weight to balance on the balls of her feet. But what if she tripped and took a nosedive at Grant's feet?

She tilted her feet from side to side to admire the design of the heels. A tightly woven lattice pattern covered the top of her foot, while her heels were bare in the slingbacks.

Without warning, Becky pushed her down on the edge of the bed. She set down her makeup bag. "We don't have much time." The transformation took exactly ten minutes. Then Becky wiped her brow, rolled up the makeup bag and motioned her to the bathroom mirror.

Tamara stared at her reflection. "Hot diggity. I like this." Tamara turned her head from side to side. Wearing makeup wasn't something new, but in her hectic life, she usually managed to put on only light foundation and lip color. Becky was able to make her look striking, giving the complete outfit a more sophisticated appeal. She glanced at the clock.

The buzz of the intercom signaled Grant's arrival. Becky left the room in a whirl of expectation.

Tamara remained in front of the mirror. It was time for her meeting with Grant. Her pulse felt like a pack of Pop Rocks, and she took a deep, unsteady breath.

"Ah, Tamara, your date is here." Becky stepped into the room with a blinding grin.

"Okay." Tamara took a deep breath.

"Wait." Becky sprayed a mist of perfume in front of her. "Hurry, walk through."

Tamara complied, feeling the perfume lightly settle on her skin. She didn't expect Grant to get close enough to appreciate the scent, but adding the extra touch couldn't hurt. Tamara took another fortifying breath before exiting her bedroom to face the man who made her feel like a shy schoolgirl on her first date.

Chapter 7

Grant had to have a date with Tamara. There was no way that he could continue in his state of mind, contemplating all sorts of sexy thoughts about her. He didn't appreciate feeling out of control, either. It was an alien state of being for him.

But he hadn't expected this attack of nerves. He felt as if he was on a prom date, especially now that he was waiting for her to emerge from the bedroom.

Usually his other dates were picked up by his driver and brought to wherever he waited. He had a limo pick up the ladies partly to impress but mostly to be emotionally distant. Taking out Tamara didn't fall under either category.

He suspected that she wasn't one to fall for his bravado. And how could he remain emotionally distant when his mind and body were in active discord with that tactic?

"Hi, Grant." Tamara emerged from the bedroom.

"Beautiful," he said. It was the first word that came to mind.

"Huh?"

"You are beautiful." He could have added a few more adjectives to completely encapsulate what he felt. But simplicity seemed to be more appropriate for this evening.

"Thank you. Shall we go?"

"Then let's go." All of a sudden, his throat was dry. Thoughts scrambled into full chaos.

"Becky, we're out of here."

The woman who had opened the door emerged from a room. She kept grinning at him, and he could only imagine what Tamara had said. Maybe he should be grateful that she wasn't scowling.

"Have a nice time, you two. Don't rush home."

Grant bit his cheek to keep from laughing. Tamara's embarrassment clearly showed on her face. He had to hurry after her as she exited through the front door.

"You have a nice place. Pretty big." He attempted small talk, hoping to ease the tension.

"I share it with my friend."

Grant noted the defensive tone that immediately colored her response. He hadn't meant to sound critical. The apartment had surprised him, with its definitely upscale zip code and expansive floor plan. Despite her involvement with helping the disadvantaged, she lived a comfy lifestyle. Nothing wrong with that, but he found it to be strangely in conflict with her attitude.

"How long have you been living there?" he probed.

"Only a year. It's a gift from my father."

"Very nice gift."

She only nodded.

He led the way out of the building to the parking garage.

"Oh, you're driving?" She looked beyond where he stood.

"Yep. I don't have any driving violations. At least not any recent ones." He grinned as he opened her door. "Don't you trust me?"

"That's a loaded question. I think it can only be answered on a case-by-case basis."

"Got to work on that," he muttered. He closed the car door and walked over to his side of the vehicle.

When he slid behind the steering wheel, his arm brushed against hers where it rested on the middle console. Even through the layers of clothing, his body reacted as if it were skin-to-skin contact. All he wanted to do was to cover her hand with his and interlock his fingers with her long, slender ones.

He half closed his eyes as he breathed in her soft scent, which evoked imagery of warm spices and tropical romantic breezes. He wanted to bathe her body with his touch. And then with his tongue he wanted to follow the scintillating path of her perfume to all its erotic points of contact.

He started the car. Its roar to life matched his internal engine, which was revved on high sexual octane. Now he had the difficult task of keeping his cool for the next three hours.

"What are you thinking about?"

"If you're going to enjoy the evening."

"I think you have a sense of what I would enjoy, what I wouldn't care to do and how I would react."

"Sounds like you're giving me a challenge…and a threat." He grinned. Suddenly testing her boundaries was quite tempting.

"Where are we going?" She looked out the window, peering up at the buildings and reading aloud the street signs. She turned a puzzled frown toward him.

"You'll see. We're almost there." Grant slowed as he approached congestion. Each block closer to his destination had more traffic and more pedestrians swarming the sidewalks and even spilling into the streets.

"The stadium, that's where we're going? Oh, my. We're going to a basketball game?"

Grant nodded. "I'm afraid to ask, but is that okay?"

"Oh, yeah. I would have never guessed. Becky and I were thinking of all the possible places." She laughed. "I didn't know what to wear."

"We'll be in the skybox. And you look great."

"*Your* box?"

"No. I don't like to spend money on things like that. But I was invited."

"So am I party crashing?"

Grant shook his head. "I was told to bring you."

"Me, specifically?"

"Yes."

"Okay, spill."

"I was talking about you a little too much. So it was suggested that I bring you along."

"Please don't tell me it's your mother." Tamara looked pained at the possibility.

"No." Grant remembered how he had felt blindsided the first time he'd met Vanessa's mother. Plus, meeting mothers was a game changer. He liked Tamara, thought she was gorgeous beyond belief, and he wanted her so badly that he couldn't walk straight. But upping the stakes with a visit to his parents was not happening. Yet. "This is a business colleague."

Tamara continued to look at him, as if waiting for him to say something else. He sensed her distrust. But he wasn't worried.

Finally, after battling with the traffic into the stadium parking lot, he parked in the VIP section and headed for the elevators. The fans were pumped for their home team, and their enthusiasm was contagious as they spilled out of their cars.

They mixed in with the hustle and bustle of fans entering the stadium. On their way to the skybox, he and Tamara chatted with strangers about the home team's overall performance for the year. Tamara offered her predictions and her tips on how the coach should proceed for the remainder of the year. He hadn't known she was a sports buff, but he had opted for this activity since it was a safe one that shouldn't make her feel uncomfortable. While he wasn't up on the latest news about the basketball world, he could hold his own at the basic level of sports trash talk.

"I didn't bother to get us refreshments because there will be food in the skybox," Grant explained as they approached the door of the suite.

Tamara nodded.

He pressed the buzzer at the suite. The door opened and the merriment from within hit them full blast.

"Looks like the party started without us." Grant stepped aside for Tamara to enter. He laid his hand gently on her back as she entered the room, and he felt her stiffen.

"Let me introduce you." Grant wanted to erase any unease she felt.

"I'm not going to remember all of these people."

"I don't know them, either." He kept his hand on her back. Little did she know that this wasn't his usual scene. He'd much rather hang out at his favorite brick-oven pizza place, but this had felt more special. And he wanted her to feel special.

"Grant, over here." His colleague beckoned to him.

Grant and Tamara squeezed through the various bodies to his colleague.

"So, is this Tamara?" His friend plunged ahead without waiting for Grant's introduction. "I'm Clinton. Thanks for getting Grant to come out and have some fun. He's such a homebody, always working on world domination." The man shook Tamara's hand and whistled appreciatively over her. "Only took a knock-out to really knock him out."

Grant had always thought Clinton was a nerd in disguise. He tried so hard to be the party guy that sometimes it irritated Grant. But to be called out about his lack of a social life by the man who had to spend tons of money to keep an entourage, well, that truly fired him up. And Tamara's laughter at his expense was a little too bubbly for his liking.

Clinton continued. "So, Tamara, what do you do? Grant seems to be scared to share any details with me."

"I run a leadership academy for teens."

"That sounds noble. Grant, why did you hide that from me?"

Grant shrugged.

"Do you find him to be very secretive?" Tamara asked, jabbing a thumb in Grant's direction. Now she was going to jump on the bandwagon to make fun of him. At least she was cute enough to get away with it.

"Always secretive. I think he likes to hold everything at arm's distance. Who knows, he might be living a double life, one for the public—hardworking, dedicated CEO—and one that's private—bargaining with the devil for world domination in the computer game industry."

"Oh, my, now that's…dark. I wonder which Grant Benson came out tonight." Tamara assessed him as if the answer would scroll across his forehead.

"I'm going to get food. I think both of you should fill your mouths, too," Grant scolded.

He didn't like being under the microscope. The media already had him there, and they didn't seem to be letting up. The constant observers kept him in a permanent state of wariness. Maybe he was being naive thinking that he could manage the situation. He excused himself and headed to the array of food that had been catered for the large crowd.

Tamara watched Grant's departure, noting the stiffness in his shoulders. Evidently Clinton had touched on a sensitive subject. At first, she had thought that Grant was playing along until she had seen his jaw working. He returned with food only for her. The easy banter was now awkward conversation. His hand, which had gently guided her into the suite, was now stuffed in his pocket. She missed the warm pressure that had gotten her hot and bothered.

"Game is about to start." Tamara stepped close to Grant and took the small plate of appetizers.

"Let's find a seat."

There were two front-row seats in the corner of the suite. People were still milling around, and with the TV monitors positioned around the room, they technically didn't have to see the game in person.

"Everything okay?" she asked, but cringed when his shoulders tensed before he shook his head. After a few minutes of silence, Tamara softly forged ahead.

"You seemed a bit put out by Clinton's comments."

"I'm fine. Clinton is right. I don't hang out. I'm pretty much a private person, and I can do without the scrutiny from within my circle and from the press."

"Not that I don't understand where you're coming from, but I think that you shouldn't change your life for others. Don't let them push you underground."

"I live a very simple life. Maybe if they did see a glimpse of a day in the life of Grant Benson, they would lose so much in ratings that they would never push another camera in my face."

Tamara listened as she bit into the barbecue wings. She hunched over the plate, hoping to keep the drippings from soiling her clothes.

"You don't get it." Tamara cleaned off her fingers and mouth. "You have too much that will hold the viewers' interest—you're a single, rich brother." She shrugged to emphasize the obvious.

"You make it sound like the price I have to pay."

"Something like that. Maybe stop trying to avoid the press, and then if you get a honey on the side, they won't care. You'd be normal and not the eccentric reclusive rich guy." Tamara tossed out the flip advice. She found it a little hard to believe that he truly stayed home.

"You've also had your share of time in the spotlight. Who do you have on the side?"

Tamara shook her head. "I used to do my share of hanging out. Got blasted as the party girl. Let me not forget—the *irresponsible* party girl. After all, my parents were serious, diligent activists, and I was taking advantage of everything they'd worked hard to achieve."

Tamara had partied, but not for attention. The partying, drinking and acting careless had all been to numb her emotions. She had lost a friend who had meant so much to her. Once the anger had subsided, she had turned her energy from self-destruction to helping others and ultimately to opening her leadership academy.

"I'm too busy all day long to have the energy to go dancing and jabbering with any guy I don't care about," she said, deflecting the question onto more neutral territory.

"What do you do with guys you do care about?"

She looked over at him. "First, I think it's more important that they care about me. If I focus on the opposite scenario—I care about the guy—then I stand to get the short end of the stick, sooner or later." She bit into another wing, feeling the sauce smear around her mouth, possibly even her cheeks. She hoped that her honesty and her lack of finesse with her food signaled to Grant that she was not "honey" material.

Suddenly, the announcer's voice boomed. "Time to

catch our couples!" The crowd erupted, along with the more noisy members in the suite. Tamara barely paid attention to the tradition.

The overhead camera zoomed in and out at various fans, showing their reactions on the big screens above the scoreboard. Some of the people weren't couples, and they waved away the camera with embarrassed grins. The crowd cheered regardless of whether the couples were real or not. The spirit of the night seemed to be celebratory.

When the camera did pick up on actual couples, the MC previewed the magic moment with exaggerated fanfare. As the fans cheered, the couples would turn and kiss, enticing the crowd to raise the volume of their screaming.

Tamara did her part with cheering. But she needed to wipe her fingers of the barbecue sauce. The stickiness was gross, and she couldn't touch anything until she washed up. She leaned forward to make her escape to the bathroom.

Suddenly, the suite erupted in raucous calls. Tamara barely made out her name being shouted. Grant grabbed her wrist and pointed toward the screen. His forehead displayed the deepest furrow that she'd seen in a long time.

She followed the direction of his pointing. Her face stared back at her from the giant stadium screens, mocking her as various emotions slid on and off her countenance. She issued a curse. Although no one could hear what she said, they could read her lips and surmise that she really wasn't saying "what the truck!"

She turned toward Grant and pulled on his arm for

him to do something. It seemed that anything she did caused an eruption of cheers.

"It'll be okay." He placed his finger against her mouth. "Shh. We can give them what they want and be done with it." He grinned as if he'd just won a prize.

Tamara blamed everything on shock. Otherwise, she would have seen the kiss coming. But nope, her brain shifted gears, sending her body out of whack.

She had been leaning for her escape to the bathroom, so Grant only had to lean in slightly. His lips connected to her mouth with a gentle touch. She felt his partly opened mouth tentatively make its acquaintance with hers. Her desire unwound as if from a slumber, slowly swirling upward toward the surface with lyrical ease, issuing its own demands. She moved in closer. However, Grant released her lips and pulled away. The warmth that had suddenly departed was replaced with the cool air of the stadium. The crowd's roar blasted into her consciousness. She swore again. The heat of desire was long gone. Now her ears burned with embarrassment.

"We'll continue this later," Grant whispered. His gaze locked on to her eyes and then her lips.

Tamara raised a shaking hand to her mouth. She kept her eyes lowered, still refusing to witness her shame on the big screen. Now she just wished everyone would stop whistling and cheering. They needed to shift to a real couple, where the kiss wasn't faked.

"There will be no part two," Tamara said flatly.

"Do you want me to prove that you're a liar?"

"Don't you even think about it."

She would stuff the chicken bones from her plate up his nose if he dared to come close again. Since apparently words had failed her, she was willing to take things up a notch and resort to physical assault, for her pride's sake.

The rest of the basketball game didn't matter. Tamara had gone to the bathroom and splashed cold water over her face. Even that hadn't worked. Once she thought about the kiss, her body heated up again as if she had come too close to the sun. The sad part was that she wanted to reach out and feel that searing heat once more. She looked in the mirror, expecting the shame and embarrassment to be evident in her face. Nothing was further from the truth. She felt alive. Her eyes were bright. She looked as if she'd gotten off a treadmill after a workout still with energy to burn.

"Are you okay?" Grant asked when she returned to her seat for a second time.

"Yes." She tried to smile at him but couldn't quite meet his eyes. "Maybe I should go home."

"Sure." He sounded off. But she had also been off, upside down, inside out for the past half hour.

This man, who was supposed to be reclusive, had taken her down a hilly path into the land of uncontrollable desire. They walked out of the suite, side by side, subdued. Tamara wondered what was next. She'd go home. They'd pretend nothing happened. Did she even want something to happen next, anyway?

Yes, her heart whispered.

No matter what she'd said, a part of her wanted to take this—whatever this was—as far as it could go. However, she really didn't have the time or inclination to be tied to a man.

A few bad relationships had soured her on the idea.

Ernie acted as if she was his sugar momma; Xavier said her net worth didn't matter, but constantly brought it up as a reason they were incompatible; and Omar's parents put an end to the relationship before it had begun because she didn't match any of their ideals of race, culture or religion. And what she'd seen time over time was that once that commitment was made, nine times out of ten the woman had to compromise her career either for marriage or for motherhood. If she refused to compromise her career, then the woman was somehow considered an unsupportive partner. As if her desires and ambitions were less important. She wouldn't hold her breath waiting for a man who could understand her conditions for a committed relationship.

"Grant?" A statuesque, well-dressed woman blocked their path. Tamara noted how winded she sounded and that her chest was heaving slightly.

"Vanessa?"

Tamara stayed silent, observing with keen interest not only the stilted exchange but also the subtle changes in Grant's body language. His jaw worked as if he were grinding his teeth on glass.

The woman had eyes only for him, and it was as if the surrounding stadium and the thousands of fans had melted away from her sight. She still hadn't looked Tamara's way. Her shocked expression had turned into an ugly mask of quiet rage.

Meanwhile, Grant stood next to Tamara as if frozen into place. Although anger didn't show in his face, he definitely wasn't a happy camper.

"I—I didn't expect to see you." The woman finally turned in Tamara's direction. "I almost fell out of my chair when I saw you on the screen. Actually, falling out of my chair wasn't quite the first response." Vanessa took a long, shuddering breath. "No, being embarrassed in front of my friends and mother was the reaction." Her fists balled at her side.

"Not here," Grant said in a quiet voice full of frost. He stepped closer to Tamara.

Oh, freakin' snap. She didn't relish going toe-to-toe with any woman over a man. Especially not his supermodel ex-girlfriend.

She felt Grant slip his hand along her back.

"Not a good idea," she muttered.

"Who is she?" Vanessa's voice barked, a little too shrill.

"That doesn't really matter. It's over and has been over between you and me. Thought I made that clear."

The woman bristled. Tears shimmered. "And is *that* why it's over?" Her eyes cut across Tamara as if she was ready to slash her to ribbons.

"Not really. I've explained it to you. And I don't plan to spend more time doing so." He pulled Tamara closer to him. She could feel his heartbeat, steady in the face of a brewing storm. Her pulse, however, was erratic, ready for a retreat. "Please, step aside. You're interrupting my evening."

Tamara exited with Grant, suddenly grateful for his hand along her back. The adrenaline that now rushed through her system left her knees weak. They headed to the parking garage in silence. She didn't feel any anger toward the spurned supermodel, although she also didn't feel sorry for her. But questions swirled over Grant's role in the breakup. And was she the rebound girl? Was he trying to make her just another notch on his bedpost? Would she be faced with the same cool, detached attitude when he was ready to call it quits?

And why was she thinking that there was *anything* between her and Grant? *Because I want there to be.*

"I'm sorry about that," Grant said. His voice sounded deep, tight and flat.

"Thank you for the apology." She waved off any further explanation. "However, we're not dating."

He said nothing as he navigated his car out onto the streets. Then he touched her hand. "I want to explain."

Tamara didn't respond. She did want to hear the explanation. But once he explained, then that would be it.

He drove away from the stadium and into northern Virginia. Tysons Corner was quiet as they drove through the streets. Grant drove until they found a twenty-four-hour diner. He pulled into the semilit parking lot, parked and turned off the engine.

Tamara gave him his space and time. They took a table in the corner of the room and ordered coffee. She waited with her hands cupped around the mug. Although the night wasn't chilly, her fingers were cold.

Grant cleared his throat and sighed. "Vanessa is my ex. A friend set me up on a blind date with her a long time ago." He made circles on the table with his coffee mug. He hadn't taken a sip since they'd had the beverages. "All the sordid details are in the news. I fancied myself in love. Thought it was mutual. She always had one hand in my pocket, and her mother's hand was in my other pocket. My parents, lawyer and friends pushed for a prenup. I argued against it. Love doesn't need a prenup."

"You have something to protect. You're creating your legacy. It's not about holding back your love for someone. At least that's my opinion." She tried to kick her soapbox under the table.

"Sounds so straightforward until emotions get intertwined."

"I think it's more than emotions, I think it's personal agendas and ambition. But I don't know a thing about Vanessa. Those are my thoughts on the matter in general."

"Won't be doing that again." Grant finally lifted the mug to take a drink.

Tamara shrugged. Whether Grant fell in love again didn't matter to her.

"You don't seem the type to take risks," she said. She imagined that he deliberated on every subject before deciding whether to proceed ahead. Except with Vanessa.

"Not usually, and I mean to stick to that rule. But with you, I went on instinct. You're like a breath of fresh air. I have no regrets."

"That's what happens when someone bulldozes their way into your world." She laughed.

"Agreed. I was enthralled by the messenger, so I enjoyed listening to the message. And now that the message has been delivered, I'm not prepared to let go."

"I will be around. Have to check in on my guys."

"Not enough. I don't want my time with you shared."

"You always want things your way?" Tamara had to admit that she liked the shift in their conversation.

"Just about."

She took a deep breath. Grant grabbed hold of her, not with his hands but with his powerful gaze. His lashes, thick and dark, framed his eyes, punctuating their mesmerizing depth. Blink, for heaven's sake. She needed release.

Tamara blinked first. "I don't have time for a relationship."

"But this will be purely business." He sipped the coffee and tossed a wink over the top of the rim.

She couldn't help but chuckle.

They eventually headed back to the car. The tension had dissipated. As he opened the car door for her, he paused and looked down at her.

"Tamara, I want to kiss you."

She reached for his shirt, balling the fabric into her fists. "Hurry up," she prompted.

He lowered his mouth to hers for a second time that night and gently kissed her lips before coaxing open her mouth. His arms wrapped her in a warm embrace. Surrendering in his arms was like falling into cotton candy, full of sweetness and decadence.

Her hands slid to his waist, holding on to his shirt to anchor her. Kissing him carried the headiness of being drunk. Her craving for him exploded until she moaned for more.

He answered her moan with a sensual caress of his tongue. Masterful strokes spoke a language of carnal intent. Every delicious maneuver hummed its own meaning.

"Tamara," Grant whispered against her cheek.

She allowed the cool night breeze to bring her internal thermometer down a degree or two. The logical side of her mind was desperately trying to intervene.

But who needed or wanted common sense at a time like this?

She decided to take the deep plunge into insanity. Standing on tiptoes, she cupped the back of Grant's head and pulled him toward her upturned face. "Kiss me again. Quick, before I change my mind."

He complied with a speed that took her breath away. His body molded against hers. His hand slid down the side of her hip, fingers curling under her butt. His arousal pressed against her.

This time, she took a tour of his mouth, enjoying the curve of his lips, claiming them. Finally, they pulled away slowly.

"So, this is the purely business part?" She bit her lip to keep from smiling.

"It's all in how you see it," he responded, with a sheepish grin. "I think that I'd better take you home."

"Yeah, for both our sakes."

The next morning, Tamara barely got to work on time. Her sleepless night had been filled with images of Grant's hot face and memories of their kisses. Her body didn't relent until the sun began its ascent. Then she fell asleep only to be awakened by a phone call from her mother.

Now at work, she wanted to rest her head on her desk and allow her body the time it needed to recuperate.

"So, how did it go?" Becky entered her office with an extra coffee mug. "I missed when you came home. I tried to wait up."

Tamara took the mug, raising it up with gratitude. "Here's the short version, and you can't ask any questions because I don't want to get into it. This afternoon Grant is coming over to meet the kids." She quickly ran through the highlights, mentioning only the one kiss—really, the quick peck—at the game. The other kiss didn't need anyone's scrutiny. That was hers to lock away in her heart.

"Cool. Okay if I stick around?"

"You don't have a choice." Tamara would love to have Becky's presence to dilute any tension between her and Grant.

"I wasn't sure that you wanted me in the middle of your reunion with Mr. Sexy."

"Oh, stop." Tamara sipped the hot drink. "The kids will be there."

"Okay. We'll see how well you both hide your thing. By the way, just a quick reminder that I'm heading to the airport afterward. Catching the eight o'clock flight out to Florida," Becky said.

"I'm jealous. The weather is supposed to be fantastic."

"Can't wait to hit the beach. I wish you could come."

Tamara hadn't taken a vacation since she'd opened the academy. "I've got too much going on. Plus, you need to be with your mom. At her age, any fall is dangerous. Fingers crossed that it's only a bruised hip."

"Probably another false alarm," Becky joked, but the worry was clear on her face.

"Maybe. But you can't be sure."

Becky nodded. "Plus, you know Denny is making a big deal that I'm not there."

"You know he's the baby of the family and he needs his big sister to take on some of the burden."

Becky rolled her eyes. "Now he has a girlfriend and she's a real pill. I think she's calling the shots."

"Uh-oh. I'm really out of the loop," Tamara said.

They chatted for a while, catching up on Becky's latest family dynamics. Tamara listened and offered advice, happy to return the favor of providing a ready ear.

"Well, whatever time you need to take care of your mom, don't hesitate to take," Tamara offered.

"Let's not jump the gun. I'm not that much of a good daughter to look forward to a lengthy stay with my mother." Becky pulled a newspaper from the crook of her arm and tossed it on the desk. "Did you read the business section? Mr. Sexy is in the news."

"Why do you have to be so dramatic? You waited until now to tell me about this?" Tamara pulled out the business section and laid it flat on her desk.

"Bottom right."

Tamara read the headline and article that had a negative spin about Benson Technologies being a rogue company that didn't have enough experience to back its risky moves.

"Wow. They don't hold any punches." Tamara refolded the newspaper and set it aside. Her academy had made it to the local news and was once featured in the county newspaper. Politicians and donors liked having photos with the kids so they could convince constituents that they were socially conscious.

Once in a while, a parent would get vocal in the media because his or her son had violated a rule and had been expelled or suspended from the program. Tamara had a three-strike rule, and she stuck to it. With those rule breakers, she wasn't a favorite. Sometimes they took their anger to social media platforms. But the rants didn't damage her reputation with local legislators; they just tended to be more of a nuisance.

The attacks also tended to be leveled at her, personally. Tamara knew that her level of social consciousness was often debated, and having parents who were heavily involved in social activism didn't help. Instead, the bar for comparison constantly shifted to make it more difficult to meet the public's elusive expectations. Her parents' success and wealth meant that she had a relatively easy lifestyle, but then again, that added a layer to the challenges that she had to overcome.

How did Grant handle the constant attacks to his vision and to himself?

There was so much she didn't know about him. After their last encounter, they had turned a corner and were now on a ride that promised to be so exciting that she wasn't ready to get off. Instead, she wanted to go around the block once more.

Chapter 8

Tamara emerged from her Grant-filled thoughts to walk with Becky to meet the students and Bill Stevenson, the director of the boys' home.

"Tamara, Becky, good to see you," Bill said.

Bill had worked his way up through the home. Together they had dealt with the learning curve and had worked to get the right candidates for the various internship opportunities. Tamara had always thought he resembled Lou Gossett Jr. in *An Officer and a Gentleman*, and she thought that his intimidating demeanor kept his young wards in line.

"Becky, do you know if Grant has arrived?"

Mitzy stepped into view after hovering on the edge of the group. "Actually, he got here about fifteen minutes ago. As soon as the guys arrived, he wanted to meet them. Mr. Stevenson thought that wouldn't be a problem."

"You're right." Tamara couldn't help but be impressed with Grant's initiative. Even Becky raised an eyebrow and nodded her approval.

Tamara led Bill to the largest meeting room. Conversation and laughter greeted their approach down the hall, and she could hear the low rumble of Grant's voice.

Just that single thought about Grant triggered her desire. Tamara couldn't stop her body's instant reaction even if she wanted to. She hated to interrupt the deep conversation they all seemed to be engaged in, so they quietly entered at the back of the room. She could hear him talking about his passion for his job. He painted such a vivid picture of his work that the kids couldn't hide their awe. His tone had an air of authority that captivated the guys. A few heads turned her way, but most of them didn't notice or didn't care that a small group stood at the back of the room, observing them.

Her gaze strayed toward Grant, and their eyes met. In the nanosecond when he looked at her, the distance between them evaporated. From the look in his eyes, she knew that he'd recognized their magnetism.

Tamara stepped up to facilitate the meeting. "Now that we are all here and introductions have already been made, what would you like to know about the guys?"

Grant looked at the youths and smiled. "We've been having a good chat. I'm impressed by their focus on what they want from this experience. I'm feeling confident that they will get it at my company."

"I can't tell you how much we appreciate you being able to take on all the guys," Bill piped in.

"I won't lie—it is a bit of a challenge." Grant laughed.

"We have faith in you," Becky said. "I'm sure that you will navigate any obstacles and transform them into one of the best creative teams under twenty-one years old. You're a man who knows how to work around obstacles, right?" Becky's compliment hovered as Tamara tried, but failed, not to read between the lines. Becky's small, impish smile was the dead giveaway that she had understood the double message.

"You give me more credit than I deserve."

"And he's humble." Becky chuckled.

"Behave," Tamara whispered, sidling up to Becky.

Becky could be quite devilish. However, now wasn't the time to push any romantic agenda. And she certainly didn't need ten students picking up on any flirtatious moments.

"Guys, good to see you." Tamara addressed the group. "I'm glad you've gotten a chance to talk to Mr. Benson."

"Grant," a few corrected.

"Grant."

"When do we start?"

Tamara looked over to Grant. "Next week on Monday." She saw his confirming nod.

The guys immediately broke into a bigger discussion. Their excited chatter increased in volume until the director clapped his hands to get them back under control.

"Do you have any questions?" She didn't want to repeat information if Grant had already told them the details.

"Is it true what Grant said?" Frederick asked.

"What did Grant say?" Tamara looked toward him for an explanation.

He shifted, clearly uncomfortable and looking a little reluctant to provide the details.

"Maybe later?" Tamara offered. She'd play along until the opportunity arose to grill him or Frederick. Knowing the young men's code of silence, she'd focus her attention on the instigator—Grant.

Grant accepted the temporary relief. Not that he didn't want to share his life story. He'd already shared it with the young men, something he didn't do readily, hoping that they could see some common points between their lives to earn him some credibility. He wanted them to understand that even though some people may have written them off, they still had the potential for a happy life. He'd never planned to be a mentor, yet here he stood already committed to their destinies. He had Tamara's brash entry into his life to explain it all.

"Guys, now, I did promise a few incentives along the way. There will be recognition for individuals, but there will be a really good incentive for the entire team. And I mean the entire team. You start with ten, and you must finish with ten. This will be testing your team-work skills," Grant said.

"Then we're screwed," Frederick, the eldest, declared. The group treated him as their leader. Grant knew he'd better learn the social norms and hierarchy of the group to get the most from them.

"Trent and Leon will mess us up," another boy volunteered.

"Man, that sucks," Graham, the youngest boy, piped up. Despite his small stature, he had quite a mouth on him. His nickname was Pint, but Grant wasn't calling them anything but what was on their IDs. It was time for the real world to step into their lives.

"Guys, what's with the attitude already?" Becky stepped up in her no-nonsense voice. "At least give this a shot."

Grant boldly stepped up. "I think, as team leader, I should get in on the incentive. I think Tamara and I should be included in the reward system."

Tamara's face flushed. "No one but the guys are getting any rewards."

Grant noted Tamara's displeasure, but he knew what he was doing. Bonding was paramount before he and the guys could start a fruitful relationship; hence, his motivation to meet them in their comfort zone. He'd tossed a few ideas out to them about the angels and demons game. They'd collectively held back, awaiting criticism or rules for how to proceed. But after much coaxing, their unfiltered imagination and unrestrained passion had had a chance to develop and bear fruit. He understood at their age how much they'd be preoccupied with other people's perceptions of them. He couldn't wait to get them into a brainstorming session with his team. They would get a chance to see how creative professionals work.

An orientation about the job and survival tips for a successful internship finished up the time that had been appointed for the guys.

"Thank you very much, Mr. Benson." Bill patted Grant on the shoulder. "You are the first owner who took the time to meet and sit with students before they go off to work." He nodded. "I'm hoping that you won't stop the internship with this group."

Grant didn't know whether to nod or shake his head. He wanted success, too, but to commit to an ongoing program was a bit premature.

Bill rounded up his ten teens and headed out to the bus.

Grant was sure to shake each person's hand as he boarded the bus. He wanted to make their lives better. With each handshake or fist bump, he forced each teen to look at him. As long as they were with him, they wouldn't hold their head down, avert eye contact or mumble their responses or requests. They would create a brotherhood by watching each other's back, lifting each other to the next level and keeping their eyes forward, not in the past.

As the bus pulled off, he was under no illusion that they would all immediately do the right thing. They would be his responsibility during the day, while still being enrolled in their alternative schools. But to be honest, he couldn't contain his excitement.

How did Tamara stay detached? He'd accused her of taking them on for personal satisfaction. Quickly he'd realized that personal satisfaction wasn't a crime. For all that he'd seen around him today, Tamara really deserved to have a sense of satisfaction.

"One stupid move by any of those guys and they could be off that yellow school bus and on a state corrections bus." Tamara sighed. She had taken the spot next to him as they watched the bus grow smaller in the distance.

An Important Message from the Publisher

Dear Reader,

Because you've chosen to read one of our fine novels, I'd like to say "thank you"! And, as a special way to say thank you, I'm offering to send you two more Kimani™ Romance novels and two surprise gifts—absolutely FREE! These books will keep it real with true-to-life African American characters that turn up the heat and sizzle with passion.

Please enjoy the free books and gifts with our compliments...

Glenda Howard
For Kimani Press™

Peel off Seal and Place Inside...

K-ROM-13B

We'd like to send you two free books to introduce you to Kimani™ Romance books. These novels feature strong, sexy women, and African-American heroes that are charming, loving and true. Our authors fill each page with exceptional dialogue, exciting plot twists, and enough sizzling romance to keep you riveted until the very end!

KIMANI ROMANCE...LOVE'S ULTIMATE DESTINATION

Your two books have combined cover pric of **$13** in the U.S. or **$14.50** in Canada, bu are yours **FREE!**

We'll even send you two wonderful surprise gifts. You can't lose!

2 FREE BONUS GIFTS!

We'll send you two wonderful surprise gifts, (worth about $10) absolutely FREE, just for giving KIMANI™ ROMANCE books a try! Don't miss out—MAIL THE REPLY CARD TODAY!

Visit us online at www.ReaderService.com

THE EDITOR'S "THANK YOU" FREE GIFTS INCLUDE:

➤ Two Kimani™ Romance Novels
➤ Two exciting surprise gifts

YES! I have placed my Editor's "thank you" Free Gifts seal in the space provided at right. Please send me 2 FREE Books, and my 2 FREE Mystery Gifts. I understand that I am under no obligation to purchase anything further, as explained on the back of this card.

PLACE
FREE GIFTS
SEAL
HERE

168/368 XDL FV32

Please Print

FIRST NAME

LAST NAME

ADDRESS

APT.#   CITY

STATE/PROV.   ZIP/POSTAL CODE

Thank You!

"That's not going to happen," he announced, even though he was feeling less confident with the guys no longer in front of him.

"Don't you two look like the doting parents?" Becky asked as she slipped in between them. "Your boys are gone only temporarily. No need for the sad faces."

"Don't you have a plane to catch?" Tamara's expression promised physical retribution. Grant did his best not to chuckle.

"Grant, I'm being chased out of my place of employment. Anyway, good to see you again. I've got to head out for a few days to deal with family. Keep an eye on our girl." Becky motioned with her chin over to Tamara.

"I'm a grown woman," Tamara protested. "Don't need anyone to keep an eye on me."

Grant raised his hands in surrender. "And I'm not about to stand in the way of that declaration."

"Whatever. You both are playing that hard-to-get game. Why? I don't know." Becky shrugged. A smug smile played on her lips.

"Good-bye, Becky." Tamara pushed her friend toward her parked car. "Have a safe flight."

Becky got to her car and turned around. "Grant, Tamara, you know this means that I'm not around to walk in on any shenanigans. Feel free." She jumped in her car as Tamara ran toward her. Grant gave in and laughed heartily at Becky's wickedly funny sense of humor.

Grant jangled the car keys in his pocket. He had managed to see Tamara two days in a row. His brain couldn't seem to come up with a proper scenario to see her for a third day.

Tamara returned from her jog across the parking

lot. Only slightly out of breath, she asked, "Would you come home with me?"

"Are you sure?" He had to ask, even if his shoulders waited to slump if she responded in the negative.

She nodded.

Grant returned the nod. Now if could get through tonight without suffering a heart attack.

He drove behind Tamara, sometimes wishing that the traffic cameras didn't impede their speed. The rush-hour traffic was some method of torture for a man who had sex on the brain. The main roads were clogged, but the side streets flowed, although the multitude of lights and cameras slowed the progress. Finally, they arrived at her place. They both found parking spots.

Grant kept his nervousness to himself. What if he said the wrong thing and this, whatever was about to happen, got shut down? Nope. He'd sit on the couch and let Tamara drive this night to whatever destination she desired.

"Make yourself comfortable." She excused herself and headed to her bedroom.

He walked to the couch and took a seat at the end. A few minutes later, he was finally able to ease back with his arm along the back of the couch. Still, he wasn't quite ready to claim any sort of calmness. Deep down he knew that he was about to cross a major milestone from which he couldn't return.

With one horrendous relationship already in his history, he didn't have any desire to get wrapped up in another emotionally draining disaster. He wasn't the type to be pessimistic, but he also wasn't the type to be delusional. No matter how many rules he had in place and how many times "no strings attached" had been declared, he had to protect himself from stepping over the line.

Tamara emerged from her room. Damn it. How could he not break his own rules when she looked like that? Dressed casually in sweats and a T-shirt that did little to hide the curve of her breasts, flat abs and curvy hips, she walked past him and busied herself in the kitchen. He listened to her preparing glasses with ice and soda.

He hadn't thought he had a parched throat until he heard the soda being poured into the glass. What was wrong with him? Here he was acting like a teenager on a first date.

"Thanks." He took the glass and took a long drink.

She sat next to him on the couch, sipping instead of guzzling her drink. "I want to propose something. I want to produce a documentary on the internship."

Grant froze with the glass in his hand. He frowned, leaning back into the couch. Nothing had prepared him for such a request—opening his life for a film.

"I know you're very private. But hear me out."

"Okay." He set down the glass but still pulled back, paying close attention. His mind struggled to switch from what his expectations had been for the night to the big, fat question about filming his life.

"I hadn't planned this idea." She turned her body toward him. "Our meeting this afternoon got me thinking. I think it's got merit, so I wanted you to hear me out."

Grant felt the shift of her body, and the small movement shook him to the pit of his stomach. Tamara had a knack for keeping him slightly off-kilter.

She continued. "I'd been reading the various reports

about you and your company. I've also been reading your biography. I know, it's not authorized, but it's a great read."

Grant resisted. "How did we get from an internship to a documentary?"

"We haven't moved from one to the other. It's still the same arrangement, only adding another element. This documentary would help you and me. Personally, I'd like to shut up some of those critics, both yours and mine."

The media circled around him, but he'd always chosen to ignore them and wanted to continue to do so. In stark contrast, Tamara seemed ready for a fight. Confidence emanated from her.

"I know a good crew that will do a bang-up job. But featuring the guys—of course, we'll go through the legal paperwork—will also highlight your company's active role in the community."

"That doesn't convince me. I don't care what people think. I'm a computer game designer."

"And the targeted end users are those kids you're mentoring. You'll want to continue with this program because it's successful," Tamara pushed.

"You can't go around manipulating people."

"I didn't," Tamara protested.

"Sorry, I'm trying to wrap my brain around this."

"But your true feeling is that I'm a manipulator," she said in a tone that was both soft and hurt.

Her hurt was now his hurt. He wished he could rewind and pull back his harsh remark.

"I can tell that you won't do it. Don't worry, I won't hold a grudge," Tamara said.

"But I put my foot in my mouth there."

"Yeah, you did." She leaned over and punched his arm playfully.

But the mood, whatever they had been entertaining between them, had cooled. Their attempt at light chatter fell flat.

"I'll head out." Grant stroked her cheek.

"See you later."

He turned and walked away. Getting used to having his head in a whirl over a woman was proving next to impossible. The way his thoughts were spinning with his insecurities and doubts was freaking him out.

This woman was quickly filling his head with delicious scenarios that may never come to fruition. Since when and how had she slipped into that role? Maybe fate wanted him to experience how it felt to want someone so much that it hurt.

"Grant."

He stopped and spun around at the sound of Tamara's voice.

She ran toward him and jumped into his arms. Her legs encircled his waist. Her mouth, with its warm welcome, covered his.

"I want to be with you."

Grant groaned.

"Stay. Please."

"You're killing me." He squeezed his eyes shut and opened them to see the wide smile that greeted him.

That smile did him in. His mouth touched hers hesitantly. Her arms gripped him harder, and he accepted the signal to proceed ahead.

Although he wanted to launch into all the things that

he wanted to do to her body, he resisted. Instead, he'd savor each moment.

His mouth slid away from her mouth, trailing down to her neck. Her slender throat was such a seductive turn on that he almost lost control. Everything about Tamara threatened his ability to stay cool and collected. He'd have to be dead to be calm.

As his hands roved over her body, warm and reactive, he could feel his pulse throbbing in response. They tore at each other's clothing desperately.

One T-shirt gone.

One dress shirt gone.

One pair of sweatpants gone.

One pair of dress pants gone.

They panted across from each other. They still stood in the living room, only a few feet away from the front door, where he had surrendered to her.

She held out her hand to him.

He took her hand and allowed her to lead him to her room. He had no illusions that she wasn't in charge, and his ego didn't mind one bit.

He would rock her world, either way.

He laid her down on her bed with his body firmly planted between her thighs. The red laced bra had to go. He slid his hand under her back and unsnapped it with a flick of his fingers. She accepted the cue and pulled it off, tossing it overhead.

Her breasts were pure delight. The brown tips were like lures casting a tightly woven net over him, leaving no chance of escape. His tongue stroked the point where her neck slid into the graceful line of her shoulder. Every angle, plane and line had to be remembered. His hand cupped her breast, massaging the delicate mound, playing with her hardened nipple. Her soft moan started deep in her throat and crept up, slowly getting louder. The vibration against his lips set off a chain reaction, starting with tiny shivers in his stomach and ending with his arousal, which was steadily growing harder.

She must have sensed his need—the urgency. Her hands pulled at her own panties. He did his best to meet the challenge *and* still keep contact with her skin.

"I had it in mind to seduce you." She handed him a condom.

He put on the protection. "I think we must have been on the same page, although mine is in my pants."

"Next time," she whispered before pulling him down on her.

He kissed her. Now that the floodgates of their desire had been opened, he plunged his tongue into her mouth as a preview for what he wanted to do with her body.

He raised her hips before sliding into the juicy cavern between her legs. Her legs wrapped around his hips, pushing up against him. The invitation was raw and hot.

He pushed back harder, grinding down and deep to fill her need. She opened herself to him, responding with a sensual challenge for deeper thrusts.

He gripped the headboard and put his strength into each stroke, mixing and matching the rhythm with hers. Their dance had a savage quality that celebrated nature in its purest form. They followed whatever their hearts desired.

Their sweat-slicked bodies worked in a frenzied partnership. Neither one wanted to surrender to the release that their bodies ached to perform. No way. He wanted more time to play, tease and seduce.

With one quick move, he flipped to the bottom and kept Tamara in place on top of his hips. She rode her position as if she was a warrior going into battle. Her arms and shoulders were back, and her breasts were up and free and bouncing with each move. Her thighs tightened around his hips as she bounced her behind against his pelvis. His legs practically shivered as she rotated and clenched her vagina around his penis. When he thought he couldn't be more aroused, she took him to another octave.

He tried closing his eyes, but he saw only stars, as if his blood had drained from his brain. Then he felt her tighten under him. He didn't need any help to know that like him, she was close to climax.

"Let's do this together," he whispered, his voice tight and hoarse.

She gasped.

Grant exploded with Tamara. His back arched up, pushing his hips into and against her. Her walls quivered, sending shockwaves along his shaft that also pulsed his orgasm. He had to surrender to his complete mental shutdown. Nothing coherent could form in his mind.

He couldn't stop grinding against her hips until the last drop had been squeezed out of his body. Then his legs felt weak, as if he'd run a marathon. Thankfully he was lying on his back. He suspected that his legs would be unstable if he tried to get up.

Even after Tamara had rolled off, he remained lying there, wondering if he needed an EKG to diagnose any heart issues. His pulse hadn't returned to normal. Maybe he needed to blindfold himself from seeing her body. But that wouldn't be enough. Seeing her was only part of his problem. Her scent was ingrained in his head. Her touch had the power to scramble everything in him, and her voice wickedly stroked him into mad cravings to be with her and in her.

Finally, after his body had returned to some semblance of normalcy, Grant propped himself up on his elbow. He looked down on Tamara lying against the pillows. Her hair fanned the pillows, and soft tendrils curled around her face. He kissed her softly on her forehead.

"Why do you blow my mind so much?"

"You have a knack for accusing me of things. But I accept the charge...this time."

Grant kissed her shoulder.

"You know I wanted to be with you. That's why I suggested the film." She cupped his jaw. "I guess I do manipulate, a tiny bit."

He kissed her forehead.

"It's no longer business as usual," she said.

"I think we've failed our trade agreement."

"So what do countries do to solve such a crisis?"

"Continue diplomatic relations." Grant pulled Tamara into his embrace.

"I'm game if you're game."

Grant didn't need any encouragement. He closed the distance between them. To have her in his arms for an encore satisfied his endless craving. While his passion still raged, he wanted to take his time with her.

They moved with the grace and timing of partners

in an erotic slow dance. She writhed under him as he tried to imprint every tantalizing detail about her body into his mind. His hands completed the rest of the orientation, smoothing over her butt, cupping each fleshy cheek with his palm. He wasn't one to claim ownership over any woman, but damn it, this was his woman.

Despite all of his plans, he'd given up more of himself than he'd intended.

He entered her with condom on, gently wanting to feel and enjoy every inch of the way. She made it hard, though. Her hips had to do just a quick flick, and he was ready to change the tempo. He held on, clenching his teeth, toes tight, brain on override as he tried to savor every movement with delicious deliberation.

"You're killing me. Shh…" she hissed, unable to finish what she was going to say.

Grant shook his head in an effort to forget her request. No matter what she said, he meant to hold on to her hips and ride the wave as long as possible. He closed his eyes to avoid looking at the swell of her breasts moving to her rhythms.

He wanted to suck on her nipples so badly.

Even that thought threw him off. He bucked for a second. Taking a deep breath, he readjusted to the rhythmic beat already in play.

Tamara moaned. In a quick and unexpected move, she slid her hand along his thigh and between their bodies. Before he could register what he was about to do, her hand closed around his balls.

He almost shot off the bed.

"Stop," he hissed. She stroked him. His voice caught in his throat. All he could do was croak.

One more stroke broke him.

He grabbed her hips and pushed forward, lifting her with his thrust. She arched back with a scream that he swore the neighbors had to have heard. But in the frenzy, he couldn't stop himself. His thrusts were thick and hard, pushing and retreating until he hit that spot that generated the quickening of her release beneath him. He waited for her to climax, and just as she was done, he surrendered, bringing her back to join him again. They played their game until exhaustion took over, and they both collapsed on the bed.

Grant closed his eyes with Tamara tucked in the crook of his arm.

An hour later, Grant got dressed. His mouth felt dry. He hated to admit that he was still suspicious that Tamara's passion for this project might have selfish motives. He walked out of the room just as Tamara was also rising from the bed.

"You're not saying anything," Tamara said. "The fact that you're keeping your back to me speaks volumes." She followed him into the kitchen, clutching the bedsheet around her body. The white linen contrasted beautifully against her dark skin. Her shoulders were bared, begging to be kissed.

"I'm still thinking about the film. Don't try to convince me why I need to do it. Instead, I want to hear what you think it'll do for you."

"Are you accusing me again? I thought we'd gotten past that." She tilted her chin toward the bedroom. "I have no personal agenda other than helping the academy so we can help more kids."

"And I'm a behind-the-scenes kind of person," Grant countered.

"You don't have to be in the film. I'm only focusing on the kids."

Grant wasn't sure how he kept getting bulldozed by Tamara. Just looking at her, with her hair mussed from their lovemaking, the sexy glow of her skin, the naked desire that was still reflected in her eyes, he knew that she had the power to knock him over, again and again.

"I can tell that you don't trust me," she said.

Grant didn't respond. His comfort zone was getting smaller and smaller.

Chapter 9

Grant couldn't deny that he had an afterglow that was lasting well into the next week. He'd caught himself whistling while doing mundane tasks. He'd found himself not only participating in office pranks, but also serving on the planning detail. His assistant, Latrice, frequently asked where the real Grant was.

His state of euphoria extended even further when the guys showed up for their jobs. Grant personally oversaw their orientation and introduction to the team of employees assigned to the internship.

He itched to call Tamara. But he forced himself to show restraint. By the end of their sensuous night together, with the documentary proposal hovering overhead, they had agreed to keep things as casual as possible.

As he walked around and talked with his staff, he

thought about Tamara's request to film these young men. No matter how much she said that she would keep him and most of his employees out of the documentary piece, he sensed that somehow she would manage to wrangle him into giving her complete access. He stood in his office and looked out over the floor. What did he have to lose?

His employees certainly didn't lack company loyalty, and moreover they were proud that they created and designed top-selling games. Their creative sanctum had been protected from the public eye. Only when the final game prototype was due to be unveiled did the camera enter the process. An introspective on him and his company could backfire. Instead of showing the company's strength, its weaknesses—young business, young owner, small staff, grudging industry respect—could come across to viewers as inexperience. The competitive nature of the industry didn't always bring out the best in others.

He turned toward his desk, where sat the final plans for the angels and demons game. They had been painstakingly reviewed by his inner staff. In his gut, he knew that once the project was complete, they would have a masterpiece on their hands. Most games had a small window of popularity, but a few managed to have a classic style that burned into people's psyche for decades. That's what he saw with the angels and demons game.

Guided by his gut, he was going to stand by this project with every ounce of his support and energy. His vision even saw the potential for a tie-in graphic novel or movie. He took a deep breath and settled behind his desk to survey the latest details.

An hour later he emerged from his office. His eyes felt bloodshot as he went around the building and viewed other computer games that were in various stages of production. Hadfield and Norton had also been sitting in his office, working out a few obstacles that challenged them. At least they had found their groove and worked well together. Their miniretreat to the golf course had proved successful, to the point that the two men had become avid golfers. He sensed a rematch on the horizon.

"Grant, we have a problem."

Whenever his PR manager, Corey Tisdale, started off their conversation with that announcement, he tensed and the beginnings of a low-grade headache automatically began to slide into place. The man wasn't known for histrionics. Grant followed him back to his office. Whatever the crisis was, he didn't need the staff rattled.

"What is it?" Grant asked with outward impatience.

"Another article was published about local companies whose CEOs were not only social outcasts, but also tightwads."

"And why do I care about this?"

"Remember, we are trying to woo some computer game creators from overseas. They are already skittish about coming to an American company. The Asian market is more attractive. We need to be squeaky clean."

"That's what I pay you to do."

"So far, so good. But we need to take the offensive. There is a self-proclaimed citizens watch group making it its business to shine the light on local companies that don't give back to the community."

"This is wasting my time."

"It's a part of doing business." Tisdale's failure to get to the point grated on Grant's nerves. "Why don't we let people know about the internship?" Tisdale asked.

"Those kids aren't to be used." Grant stared at Tisdale until the man lowered his eyes. "Did Tamara put you up to this?" Grant's temper heated up with an intensity that was ready to burn out of control.

"Who?"

"Never mind." Grant was losing his mind thinking about it.

Grant paused on his way to the door. He still bristled under the thinly veiled criticism. All he wanted to do was create his games. He picked up the newspaper, scanned the contents and then tossed it aside.

"Sir, I know you don't want to hear this, but it won't go away. I have a few sources who confirm that people will jump on the opportunity to blow this out of proportion. You are a giant in the industry and you have an Achilles heel or two."

Grant nodded. "I'll get back to you." He left the office without waiting for an acknowledgment.

His cell phone vibrated in his pocket. He pulled it out and saw the familiar number. After the conversation he'd just had, he had no desire to go down the same road with anyone, including Tamara. He pressed the ignore button.

According to his schedule, he had a meeting with a couple of graphic artists who had studios in the local area. He didn't know if he'd ever use them, but he always kept his options open. Networking was another facet of the job that he enjoyed, especially if it was with industry professionals instead of the "civilians." He headed out of his office to his car.

As he came through the main entrance, he was suddenly stunned by cameras snapping in his face. He was blinded by their flashes, and all he heard was his name being yelled at him in a disjointed chorus. The security guards attempted to keep the reporters out of his path.

Navigating the gauntlet of journalists proved difficult. Was all this mayhem the result of the newspaper article? Did people have nothing better to do than invade his privacy with stupid questions?

His phone buzzed again. He looked down at the incoming number. This time he answered, ready to talk to Tamara.

"Hey, just wanted to give you a heads-up about a news—"

"I know." He cut her off, instantly regretting that it sounded curt.

"I know you're busy."

"Yeah, I'm heading to a meeting, but I always have time to talk to you." Grant left out that reporters had draped themselves over his car.

"Well, I just wanted to see how you were doing."

Grant tapped the phone against his temple, right at the spot where his headache seemed to thrive. He emitted a groan before returning the phone to his ear. "I've changed my mind. You may produce the documentary, but I want a say in the final cut." His teeth gritted in frustration.

"Whoa! That's a big change." Her voice held a tinge of disbelief. "You're a stubborn man. Why the change?"

"I thought about it and, well, your argument made sense."

Two hours later, Grant sat in Tamara's office repeating his decision.

"Okay, where's the real Grant?" Tamara walked around the room, opening and closing doors, pulling aside the blinds. "Someone come get this impostor."

"Keep it up and I'll change my mind."

"Spoilsport."

Grant pushed aside the humor. "I know you've thought about the details, so fill me in with the what, when, where and how."

To her credit, Tamara got straight to the point. She fed him all the information. He listened attentively, peppering her with questions only when some detail made him uncomfortable.

"How soon can you get started?"

Her eyebrows popped.

"You have every detail ironed out, so I'm figuring that you're ready to fly with this." Grant wanted to see her commit, but more important, he wanted the project to be done with the highest quality.

She nodded. "It will only take one phone call." She gazed at him.

His agitation increased. "What?"

"Nothing."

"Weren't you the one hounding me to do this?"

"Asking. Suggesting. Recommending. But, hounding—that's a bit much." She stepped back, resting her hip against the wall. Her expression showed how much she was interested in what he said.

"I don't want to take advantage of the guys." And somewhere not too deep under the surface, Grant knew that was exactly what he was doing.

"I don't think you would do that."

"You'd suggested that I should be putting on a different face for the media. What does that involve?"

She nodded. "But you look like you've had to swallow a bitter pill to agree to the film. If you're hesitant or unconvincing, that will come through on screen. Then you'll be faced with a bigger problem—damage control."

Grant said nothing.

"Is there anything that you'd rather not come out under public scrutiny?"

"No."

"Okay," she said quietly.

Grant stepped away from Tamara. This plan to keep her in his close circle should work, and it would also get the media off his back. Increasing the good press for the internship program would help all involved. Yet, he felt as if he'd walked in mud up to his knees to make this happen.

"You worry too much," Tamara scolded. "You've got so much stuff locked up in that head." She laughed, no humor lacing the sound. "The entire world isn't your enemy."

Her message came through.

They were already lovers. Since when was that enough to hold a relationship together, though? Lovers betrayed each other all the time. Witnessing and living through betrayal left the soul a minefield.

He wrenched his gaze away from Tamara. Her soft sigh did even more damage; it was as if she had hit him squarely between the shoulder blades. *She wasn't the enemy.* His heart had made its declaration. But it did have a track record for faulty logic.

Tamara clapped her hands together. "Let me get on the phone and get the ball rolling. Then we can meet with the crew and talk about specifics," she said in a crisp, all-business tone.

"Sounds good."

Tamara walked to her desk and sat. Her face was stoic, giving away nothing. They said a quick good-bye and he took his exit.

Outside her door, he exhaled. A burden had been lifted, somewhat. The bad publicity against his company and his plans would be averted. He had to save what he'd built at any cost. His gut did its tap dance with indigestion. He popped an antacid and headed for his car.

Tamara had gotten what she wanted. Filming Grant in his surroundings, sharing his passion and presenting his vision, had quickly become her main goal. From the first time she'd met him, he'd had a unique ability to draw her in. And she didn't count herself as someone who easily fell for a handsome face or even charming manners.

Grant had that "it" factor that caused everyone to want to be around him. She'd seen it with his employees. She saw it when they went out on their dates. She saw it with the young interns. But Grant never showed that he needed that stroke to his ego. If anything, he almost seemed bashful at the attention.

And yet, what did she really know about him? The media had touched on some of the sides of Grant that she wondered about, but she'd like to think that she didn't believe some of the negative hype.

Liar.

Her cheeks burned with the thought that she did have reservations about Grant, especially his wealth and his motivation for doing what he did.

The next day, Tamara placed the last of the follow-up calls to set things in motion. She couldn't help the excitement that was stirring into existence. Despite her curiosity about him and his company, he had nothing to fear from her motives.

By the time she hung up from the call, her writing pad was filled with pages of how the production would unfold. Little by little, she mapped out the story line, making sure to add pieces that highlighted the guys but that also detailed Grant's personal involvement with them.

He had to come across as a man who was ready to roll up his sleeves and work; a man who wasn't afraid to sit down among his employees and build something into a much-coveted product; a man who wasn't so full of his success that he couldn't reach out to be an inspiration to others.

Once she was satisfied with what she'd written, she emailed it to the head of the film production crew, copying Grant on the email. She didn't want to spring anything on him. His feelings mattered to her, despite how suspicious he had been when she'd briefed him.

Her cell phone buzzed—Becky.

"What's up?" she greeted.

"You're sounding way too perky. I thought you'd be upset that I was gone for a bit longer than I said," Becky said.

"I am. But I don't want you rushing from your mom's side. How's your mother?"

"She's not doing as well as expected. The fractured hip is now their main concern. Once she's stable, they will deal with the pacemaker. She's on complete bed rest, not that she has a choice."

"I'm so sorry. I'll keep her health in my prayers." Tamara dreaded what Becky would undoubtedly tell her next.

"I'm going to stay here. I have no idea about anything right now."

"Hey, don't worry about us here. Clear your head of this place. Okay?" Tamara's stomach clenched. Becky was her right-hand woman. "Take as long as you need. Keep me in the loop, and pass on my love to your mom."

"Thanks, Tamara. I'm so freaked out by everything."

"By the way, what does your brother think?"

"He doesn't have a say because his girlfriend is acting as if she's his wife and she's ruling the homestead. But I want to concentrate on making our mother as comfortable as possible. More than likely I will have to put her in a senior home. Not my favorite choice, but it's that time in life to make the difficult decisions."

"I understand." Tamara pinched the bridge of her nose. Listening to Becky talk about her mother reminded her about how difficult it had been with her father. "Take care of your mother."

"Thank you. I could just hug you."

"I miss your hugs, too."

"Hey, how is it going with your boy toy?"

"I will pretend that I don't know who you are talking about." Tamara filled her in on the documentary and updated her on the various stages of production.

"I'm impressed. You have way more sway than I thought you had over Grant. You are a woman of hidden talents. Or you're relentless as heck and he couldn't take your badgering anymore."

"You're lucky that you're thousands of miles away. I can't strangle you."

Becky laughed.

"Time for me to get back to work. Time for you to go check on your mother. Give your brother a hug."

"One out of the two requests is doable. That last one you may have to pay me."

This time it was Tamara's turn to chuckle.

"With all seriousness, Tammy…"

Tamara knew that when her friend used her childhood nickname, they were communicating on a deeper level, like sisters. They had gone through a heck of a lot through the years.

They had been there for each other as they dealt with boyfriend breakups, breast cancer health scares and workplace drama.

Becky restarted. "Look, Tammy, staying here with my mother has made me think a lot about my mother's health, my own mortality, the family that I really want to have. Sometimes, it's good to slow down to really live."

Tamara heard the message and she even agreed with Becky, but only when it came to Becky's life. She operated under a different set of rules. Slowing down wasn't a solution for her.

Becky continued. "I like Grant. Because I'm a spectator, I can see ahead of you. If you'd bother to open your eyes and heart, whatever you're running from or wherever you're trying to go wouldn't matter. Don't let fear overtake you." Becky paused. "Are you listening to me?"

"Uh-huh." Tamara didn't want to wander down the romantic road that Becky used to navigate her own life. She wasn't a total skeptic on love, although marriage did require a bit more effort than she was willing to provide. But the expectation that she would go after Grant for marriage was not only a bit premature, but highly unlikely given their mutual views on the matter.

"I hear the wheels turning in your head," Becky said.

"Leave me alone, woman."

"Please tell me that you haven't already ditched the man and moved on to someone else. You need to give this man a chance. I can feel that he's the right one for you."

"What pills are you taking? I'm not trying to get attached to anyone. My left ring finger will be void of any jewelry for a long time, and I've taken a blood oath to that, in case you didn't know."

"One day you'll wake up."

"Doubt it, because I'm already awake and seeing the world just fine."

If, and that was a big if, Grant and she ever got together in a serious way, he had to know from the start that she wasn't willing to play Tammy, the happy wife and housekeeper.

"You know, sometimes Tamara doesn't always know what's best."

"Why are you so stressed about me and Grant? A month ago, we were on the same page." *About hating men,* she wanted to add.

"I met someone."

"When? Why are you holding back on me? I should have known. Okay, 'fess up."

"I met a guy who is in a band."

"What the hell?" Tamara rolled her eyes. She could see the drama already starting for Round One. She didn't know if she had the stamina for all ten rounds, especially when she'd be the one to pick up the pieces for Becky.

"His name is G-Dragon," Becky announced with a dreamy lilt in her voice.

"Oh, no."

"What?"

"G-Dragon! What the hell? Where did you meet Mr. Dragon?"

"Stop being a nit. That's his stage name. He's in a hip-hop group. I first saw him perform over the summer at the international rock festival in New Jersey."

"That one? The group you dragged me to see in the fall?"

"Yep."

"Oh, my God, not the Asian dude with blond hair and tats? I knew we shouldn't have bought the VIP tickets!" Only Becky could make a backstage encounter more than a normal fan meet and greet. She should have known that the small-framed, bad boy type would have ensnared her friend.

"South Korean to be specific," Becky corrected.

"Whatever. I—I don't know what to say. He's not even local, as in not a citizen of the U.S. of A."

"Don't you think we know that?"

"Are you using your mother's illness as an excuse? Are you with him now?" Tamara hated to think that she'd been duped.

"Give me some credit."

"Why should I? You kept this a secret for several months." Tamara didn't try to hide her disappointment.

"Sorry, but I knew you'd lecture me, so… Anyway, he's coming back through the area in the fall. Then, we'll see how it goes."

"I'm *supposed* to lecture. That's what BFFs do. I'm glad that I still have several months to pull you off that romantic cliff."

"I'm not you, Tammy. I need someone in my life. Not to make me complete, but because I'm not afraid to open my heart and feel and respond."

"Also to have that heart broken."

"I don't have the energy to walk around waiting for the world to come crashing down on me or to expect the worst from people."

"Don't try to make me out to be the party pooper." Tamara smarted under the criticism. "Let me know how your mom is doing and whatever you need worked out on this side of the world."

Her friend sighed. "Okay."

After the call ended, Tamara sat back, trying not to nurse the feeling of abandonment. Somehow she felt as if Becky had pulled up stakes and they were no longer in their girl-independence mode together.

Tamara had to admit that she sometimes took Becky's presence for granted. After high school, they had gone off to college together and then declared New York City their city of choice to start their careers. They'd leased an apartment that had sucked their finances dry. In the Big Apple, they'd embarked on the dating scene, casting themselves as the fresh faces of *Sex and the City,* only to come out with bumps and bruises to their egos. Finally, after an especially disastrous double date and too many cosmos to count, they'd declared that New York City had won. They'd headed back home to northern Virginia to reenergize and settle into a new groove.

During that time of self-discovery, Tamara had thought she could erase her past. But she couldn't let go; she couldn't move forward. The young man who had intersected her life with sad brevity still haunted her years later. Deep within her heart, regret and guilt lingered. So, outwardly she pretended everything was all right and refocused her energy on the kids at the academy.

Now her best friend might as well have run off with the circus. How could she hook up with a Korean musician named G-Dragon? The scenario was laughable. Once she was done with the documentary, Tamara had all intentions to intervene, even if Becky pitched a fit.

Unlike Becky, she could work and be around a man without falling for him. Grant may be a hottie. He may have a drop-dead gorgeous smile. He definitely could make her blush with his lovemaking skills. But she could take the witness stand that she had no deep feelings for him. Because whatever feelings stirred to life at the thought or sight of him couldn't possibly be attributed to falling in love.

Chapter 10

Three weeks later, after much haggling over what would be covered in the minidocumentary on Benson Technologies, the film production had officially begun. Grant watched the film crew march in and take over his house. Tamara was nowhere in sight, which raised his anxiety level. Maybe it was a good thing for her that she was unreachable. This disruption was beyond anything she had described. So much for her Excel spreadsheet filled with false information.

A bulky lighting device hit his living room wall as two men struggled unsuccessfully to maneuver through the area. Recent rain showers had softened the dirt outside, and now the crew was tracking in mud on his wood floor. Grant swore with a ferocity that caused a lull in nearby conversations. His patience had withered down to a frail thread promising to snap at any moment.

To the workers' credit, they apologized profusely, but Grant only raised his hand to signal that all was okay. Whenever he passed, they'd stop what they were working on to apologize. By the third round of apologies, Grant had had enough. Instead of using the path through the living room, he took a longer way around to avoid their penitence.

"Mr. Benson, if I may have a moment," said a young woman in a crisp suit. "While the crew sets up, let's run through the interview."

"Sure." He turned his attention to the young lady, who was looking efficient with a writing pad in hand.

"Tamara said we should go with a soft look. Could you change out of the black shirt and go with a pastel polo shirt?"

"But this is what I wear to work. It's my uniform. Everyone knows that I wear black on black and black athletic shoes." He kicked out his foot to show the proof.

"This isn't just a run-of-the-mill story, Mr. Benson." Her voice dropped a tone as if she was addressing a wayward child on the playground. "The wardrobe is important for the visual impact."

"Ah, Wendy, I'll take this from here." Tamara walked up and interjected herself between him and the woman. "I promise to bring him back in one piece and dressed in the right clothing."

"Is that so?" he growled, less from irritation and more from wanting her. They had had small meet-ups, a mixture of romantic dates and torrid sexual throw downs, but those were frustrating because they were both busy and it was difficult to squeeze in real quality time to see each other. Now just the sight of her made him both aroused and crabbier than before.

How could a woman walk into a room and the first thing he thought about was having sex with her?

And why not?

She took his hand, pulling him up the stairs. He loved how determined she looked, as if she were ready to take on the big bad ogre and battle over the color of his shirt. Well, she could play stylist if that was her thing. He planned on playing something a bit more primal, more hedonistic.

"Why are you being such a pain in the rear?" Tamara asked, once they were in his bedroom.

"I was simply stating a point of fact to Wendy, if she had bothered to listen."

"You want to be ornery. I saw you have a fit when the guy hit the wall with the lights."

Grant hit the door shut with the heel of his boot. "He almost took out a chunk of my wall."

She looked at the closed door and then at him. A slow grin crept over her face. She shook her head, already reading the naked desire in his eyes that he hadn't bothered to hide.

"Maybe I need to be punished."

"Don't tempt me."

He pulled her close against his body. "Or else…"

"You're so baaaad." Her mouth opened slightly over the vowel. The sight of her tongue shot electric volts straight to his arousal. "And you're so hard." Her hand cupped him with a slow stroke that had the power to weaken his knees.

"Damn, woman, you are dangerous for my health."

"Sit down." She pushed him back onto one of the armchairs in the room.

"You are so bossy."

"Only when necessary."

"And you count this as one of those times?" He reached for her face. He wanted to pull her closer and take claim to her mouth. But she wasn't playing nice. Her intent stare into his eyes told him that she wasn't going to be playing nice for the next few minutes.

She placed her foot on his thigh.

"Pull down my hose."

He slowly slid his hand from her ankle, over her calf, past her knee and along her thigh. He found the garter clip and unfastened it without taking his eyes from her face.

Without prompting, he performed the task on the other leg. This time his fingers lingered at the top of her thigh.

Her breathing hitched and she didn't exhale until his hands returned to their original mission and removed the hose.

"Were you planning to seduce me?" he inquired. The answer didn't matter.

He rested one hand gently against her inner thigh. With deliberate intent in his wandering fingers, he mounted an ascent up her leg.

His body hardened, ready for the treasure hunt that his fingers sought.

There.

His fingers brushed the moist lips of her vagina. She wasn't wearing panties. Her wicked smile let him know that she had planned this all along.

She wiggled her hips ever so slightly, greeting his fingers with her sign of welcome—her moistened clit.

He played, fingering the sensitive nub and the inner and outer folds as if she were his musical instrument, warming her up for the perfect-pitch performance.

Her slight tremor and soft moan coaxed him to the next level.

Grant quickly undid the zipper on her skirt. The sight of her triangular gift made his arousal lurch. But he wasn't ready to give in just yet. Not before he had a chance to savor and explore her with his fingers, then his tongue and then his penis.

The fantasy sucked his breath away. The reality gave him energy. In one smooth move, he stood and flipped her onto the chair, spreading her legs wide for his enjoyment.

"What about the crew downstairs?" she asked.

"They can't join in." Grant's mock outrage earned him a soft punch to the chest.

"Wendy's waiting for you to change."

"And it's taking me a while. So, sue me."

"They are getting paid by the hour." Tamara moaned as his fingers stroked her in all the right places.

His eyebrow cocked.

"I'm sure this was exactly what was on your mind when you came through the door today. I could smell that you wanted me."

"You're too arrogant for your own good." She ran her hands over his head, stroking his ears, pulling softly on the lobes.

Grant leaned forward and blew softly on her clit.

Her hips shifted upward, seeking more from him. He was glad to oblige.

He repeated his cycle of blowing soft whispers of breath on her clit, teasing the sensitive folds with his fingers and probing her with his tongue until she creamed.

Every part of her was beautiful, and her natural wetness upon his finger's entry delighted him. It was as if her body was screaming that she wanted him to make love to her.

"Still think I'm arrogant?" He only barely removed his gaze from between her legs to her face before returning his full attention to her natural treasure.

Her fingers curled along the armrest, the tips digging into the fabric. Her neck arched and her hips rocked up and back in a dance with his fingers.

"My hair will be a mess," she hissed.

He kissed her clit.

"I'm going to be so embarrassed." She sighed.

"Embarrassed is if I make you scream so loud that they hear you."

She instantly stilled. Her anticipation thrilled him.

His tongue and teeth worked in tandem. First, he bathed her with long, deep strokes before he sucked her sensitive lips between his teeth.

The first time, she moaned. She practically bit her lip to keep the sound muffled.

Grant took it up a notch after her natural juice had lubricated his fingers. His exploration into the cave between her legs continued as he massaged and coaxed her body's response. He watched her closely for the point when he hit her G-spot. He watched for when she couldn't hold on, couldn't hold back and had to let go.

Her body twitched, and he continued waking up its secret paths until he heard her sharp inhalation. Pressing into her with his fingers, he raised up from between her legs and covered her breast with his mouth. He sucked while stroking and adding pressure to both sensitive points. She arched back, frozen into a contorted position, a guttural groan escaping into the vast room. She stayed in suspended animation for several seconds before her body relaxed in his hands.

Tamara couldn't believe that she'd gotten the booty call she'd craved, but now the entire house would know. Grant and his magic fingers had taken her on an out-of-body experience, and she was sure she'd lost consciousness at some point. He would not stop grinning as she slowly put on her clothes.

In the throes of her passion, she'd had no ounce of shame. With the crew working just one floor below, she didn't know how she'd face them.

"Stop looking so freaked out. At least you managed to get me into the blue shirt." Grant took a deep breath and plunged into the deep end. "I want you to have a key to the house. Actually, it's a code, but...yeah."

"Oh." Tamara took the paper on which he'd scribbled numbers and letters. "Big step."

"For big feet." He winked, before planting a hot, juicy kiss on her mouth.

Tamara squeezed her eyes shut. Her craving for this man was beyond unbearable. Of course there was the addictive sexual side to their relationship that reminded her of her womanhood. But now a softer, more vulnerable place was also opening up within her. As much as she needed the physical tango of their flesh touching and orgasms firing off, she found that she also craved being in Grant's arms, sharing their thoughts and feelings, opening up to each other for comfort. It was a romantic feeling that she hadn't realized she wanted.

The word *romantic* had been a dirty word in her vocabulary. Yet every moment that she spent with Grant changed her. He had the power to knock down wall after wall of her defenses.

At this rate, she was screwed.

They rejoined the crew downstairs. Grant headed down first, while Tamara followed several steps behind, self-consciously smoothing her hair into place. No one seemed to notice their extended absence. Instead, Wendy approached him with an approving grin over his choice of the pastel blue shirt.

"How am I doing?" Grant asked between takes.

"Fine." Tamara hadn't been paying attention, but she had already seen him in action in front of the camera. Once he had the key points of the topic, his natural talent for public speaking took hold.

"This has turned out to be a lot of work. Seeing things behind the scenes gives me a new perspective on documentaries." He surveyed the area still littered with the equipment. They had one more day of filming at his home before turning their attention to the company.

Tamara nodded.

"Stick around." Grant moved through his living room, adjusting decorative items, straightening furniture and shifting rugs.

"Are you asking me?"

"Why should I? You can stay if you want or leave if you want."

She walked over to her pocketbook.

"Was that the wrong answer?"

"I guess today it is." Tamara adjusted her bag over her shoulder. She joined in with the crew, who also prepared to depart. Discovering the depth of her new feelings for Grant rattled her. Maybe the feelings were one-sided. Grant didn't seem to care one way or the other whether she was around. Now every move he made, anything he said, she would second-guess.

By going against her desire to stay, she felt emboldened and strong. She had to prove that walking away from him wouldn't kill her.

Oprah would be proud.

But why did she feel like crap? She exited the house and headed to her car. Her keys dropped out of her hand as she tried to unlock the door. She was determined to brave it out.

"Tamara, would you stay for dinner?"

She inserted the key into the lock.

"Please."

She turned the key.

"I want you to come back."

"Why?"

"Well, my mom just called from the main house and said that I couldn't come back until you came to the house."

Tamara stared at Grant's reflection in the window. Was he kidding? No smile broke his countenance.

"I can't go back in there without you," Grant declared.

Tamara turned and rested her hips against the door.

"Meeting parents is a big deal. I don't take that lightly."

"Nor do I." His gaze went deep in her soul.

"Really, from the confirmed bachelor?" Tamara mocked.

"It's only a dinner."

"But it's your parents."

Grant nodded. "It's another milestone," he declared. "Are you okay with that?"

Tamara paused and looked at him.

"Yeah, I think that I am." Tamara locked the car and headed back toward the house. She took Grant's offered hand. For the moment, the waves of tension had quieted. They'd face the next challenge together.

"We can head over to my parents' in an hour."

"Now I'm nervous. I hope that your mother's not going to too much trouble." What was his mother expecting? This sounded like a command performance.

Grant shrugged. "She's the type who would wear a huge Easter hat on any day of the week, if the mood hits. She marches to her own beat. The family story is that she proposed to my father. What you see is what you get with her."

"Sounds like she's got a lot of energy."

"To put it mildly. Stay strong…I got your back." Grant smiled and playfully nudged her ahead of him.

Chapter 11

Tamara entered Grant's house for the second time that day. As the last SUV filled with crew members left the premises, the bustle that had surrounded the area was now gone. The quiet that always seemed to infiltrate and take over the space resettled over the house. Even his housekeeper moved through the rooms on whisper mode. Grant excused himself while she stayed put in the living room.

The tall cathedral ceilings allowed streams of natural light to illuminate the rooms. She loved that, besides refurbishing the floors and adding a few built-in bookcases, Grant had maintained the integrity of the Tudor-style guest home.

The house had four bedrooms with six full bathrooms. Grant had managed to hold on to his bachelor-style decorations, with computers and various related gadgets overtaking nearly all the rooms, except the living room and his bedroom.

"We have to wait to be summoned." Grant walked into the room, dressed as if he was going to a business-casual event.

"Well, if you're getting dressed up, so am I. I think I have a few clothes in your closet."

"Just hurry." Grant looked at his watch. She'd seen him this tense only when the film crew had started filming. She quickly changed and joined him again in the living room.

"What shall we do while we wait? Hey, I've got a fun activity." Tamara laughed.

Grant shook his head vigorously. "This time we keep our clothes on."

"Just kidding." Tamara raised her hand to halt any further protest. "I'm going to see your mother, and I don't want her to pick up on anything."

"Good. Because my mother always knows stuff before I tell her."

"Okay, your mother is sounding like I may need to be worried. What about your father?"

"Oh, he'll love you." Grant looked up. "Not that my mother won't."

"Yeah, right." Tamara exhaled. Why had she agreed to this torture?

"How about we play checkers?"

"I'm not good at that," Tamara complained.

"Great. This will be the redo of our golf challenge."

Tamara laughed at Grant's tenacity. If winning at a board game would rebuild his ego, then she was willing to play along.

They played two games, and she won both. They started in on a third game.

"I think you lied to me. You do know how to play." Grant pushed his piece across the checkerboard. His new position on the board was a neutral spot. He studied the board with such intensity that Tamara couldn't help but chuckle.

"I didn't say that I didn't know how to play. I just said that I'm not good."

When it was her turn, Tamara studied the board and shifted her piece to the left. She spied the line to the king position.

Grant moved another piece.

She allowed her gaze to rest on his progress, noting that with another move he could shift into position to take out two of her pieces.

However, she still had that path that would take her straight to the crowning position. She smiled. He would have to come up with another challenge. The game would be over in a snap.

But only if she moved that piece down the diagonal path.

She hesitated, and finally she moved a different piece.

Grant pushed his piece into another spot, blocking any chance she had to stop his advance to be crowned.

Tamara almost wanted to wipe away his smug smile. But she had no desire to kill his joy over winning, especially since she knew she had made it easy for him.

He pulled her chin toward him and kissed her mouth. "Congratulations to me. I'm the greatest." He winked. "Go ahead, agree with me."

"Is this how you ended up a computer nerd? The neighborhood kids booted you out of the sandbox and sent you packing to play with your computer in your room?"

His smiled vanished. "Now that's just cruel." He kissed her again. "But yes, that sounds right."

"Now we're even," she said.

"We've always been even, which is why I like you."

A compliment had never boosted her spirit as this one did. More than boosting her spirit, his declaration lit hope in her heart because she could see his sincerity.

"It's time." Grant looked down at his watch.

The declaration might as well have been cold water dousing her. Tamara stepped away from the checkerboard and headed for the nearby mirror. She styled her hair and freshened her makeup. Not that she expected the matriarch to do a body check, but she made sure to wear underwear and hosiery with no snags.

Becky would be over-the-moon happy to see her acting like a young teen going out with her first love.

Love?

"Oh, hell no," she muttered under her breath.

"Excuse me?"

"Nothing. I'm all set." She stood, still overcome with a case of jitters. "Heading to the bathroom."

Tamara closed the door and took a moment to calm her nerves. Had she trapped herself? What had happened to blocking out Grant's sexual power?

Instead she seemed to be soaking up every ounce of whatever sexual energy he exuded. Now she was going to meet his mother. A meeting of that magnitude required days, not one hour, of preparation. She got small comfort from observing Grant's nervousness. Normally, she'd find that funny and tease him. But if he was this nervous about meeting his mother, then she should be petrified.

She really wanted to see how Grant worked his charm between the two parents. So far, he seemed to be a big mama's boy. She hoped that Mama Bear didn't approach in full defense mode over her son. What if she wasn't considered good enough?

Good enough for what, though? Girlfriend? Lover? Bride? How much sway did Mama Bear have?

Tamara wet her fingers with cold water and touched her cheeks and neck. It helped cooled down the intense debate that raged within her head. Time to go and face the unknown.

They walked from the smaller house to the large family mansion under the brilliance of the late-afternoon sun. She was grateful for Grant's hand holding hers. He definitely appeared nervous. They both remained quiet as they strolled, lost in their own thoughts.

Humidity hung in the air as heavy as their silence. She didn't know what Grant was thinking at the moment. She was determined to remain smiling and to work at being lighthearted.

Flowers always lifted her mood, and Grant's property had amazing gardens. Various shades of green, lush and vibrant, covered the vast property. Whether planned or not, flowers grew out of rocky formations in wild assortments of vivid colors. With the backdrop of the vivid green carpet, the landscape had a British garden feel, full of magic and beauty.

They left the graveled footpath and walked up the

steps leading to the door. When they hit the last step, the door opened.

"You're late." A tall older woman who bore a resemblance to Grant peered down at them.

"Uh-oh, how late am I?" Grant tapped the face of his watch.

"One minute, twenty seconds."

"Tamara, this is my mother, Martina Benson."

"Hi." Tamara weighed the consequences of fleeing the scene.

"Come in." His mother closed the oversized front door. Tamara's nerves were now getting the better of her. She'd worked hard to stay calm, but Grant wasn't helping with his own obvious anxiety.

With a slight pressure on her elbow, Grant guided her through the house. This walk felt like a death march into the unknown. It certainly didn't help that Grant didn't seem to know what to expect, either.

She looked up at his profile.

Maybe he did know. She couldn't possibly be the only woman who had been brought before his mother. Was this how a new princess in England felt being led to Queen Elizabeth? She hadn't practiced a curtsy since her high school ballet production.

"Now that we are all here." His mother was now all smiles.

Tamara almost felt the need to bob at the knee in a curtsy. Instead, she shifted from foot to foot and gave his mother a quick handshake. "Good evening, ma'am."

The shrewd woman assessed her with a frank gaze that scoured her from top to bottom. Although Grant did have a gaze that could rip someone to shreds, he always maintained an approachable demeanor, unlike his mother.

"Have a seat, Tamara, over here," his mother said.

Tamara wasn't going to refuse the softly spoken request. If she did, however, it would have been difficult since the older woman had her wrist in a viselike grip.

"Grant, you sit over there."

"Why are there extra place settings?" he asked.

"I invited a few friends." His mother turned to her. "Would you like a soft drink?"

"Water is fine." Tamara stood behind her chair, waiting for the order to be seated. A small trickle of sweat rolled down her back. It was going to be a long night.

Meanwhile, Grant was suddenly a picture of relaxed elegance, and she wished that he wouldn't be so at ease. Why should she be the only one suffering?

The doorbell sounded. A blend of voices, male and female, rolled into the dining room. Tamara made out Mrs. Benson's voice greeting the new guests with a thousand percent more enthusiasm than she'd used to greet her.

Tamara faced Grant at the opposite side of the table. His attention was at the door. His forehead was deeply furrowed.

There was a lull in the conversation in the outer room, and the most distinctive female voice reached her.

Tamara's eyes popped open. She held on to the back of her chair. What kind of blindside was this?

"Tamara, darling, isn't this a wonderful surprise?" said her mother as she strolled into the dining room.

"Not really, Mom." She hugged her mother.

"Oh, stop it. You're so bad." Her mom hugged her

again. Unlike Mrs. Benson, her mom was a bundle of warm energy that reached out and enveloped a person.

"When Grant told me about you, and that was only because he slipped up, I realized that I knew your mother." Mrs. Benson's icy attitude seemed to have warmed up a few degrees.

"We play tennis at the club once a week," her mother said with a light, charming laugh.

Oh, joy! This definitely put a new kink in the night. Her mother didn't need to be involved in her personal life. But it was too late. Nothing could pry her mother off this trail.

"Grant, you are quite handsome," her mother said.

Realization hit Tamara.

This *was* a setup.

From the look on Grant's face, he had also come to the same realization.

"Sit. Sit. Your dad is the one who's whipping up tonight's dinner."

"What?" Grant's mouth actually dropped open.

Tamara obeyed the directive to sit just to give herself something to do. Otherwise, she'd remain gaping at her mother.

On cue, an older man came through the door with a silver platter in his hands.

"Dad."

Tamara had thought he was the family's chef, but the revelation that the patriarch had entered the room captured her full attention.

His father proudly set down the dish. "Hello, folks. This is a new recipe from my stash."

"All of a sudden your father has turned into the Renaissance man." Mrs. Benson rolled her eyes. "He won't let anyone help him. He shouldn't be carrying that tray."

Despite her comments, Grant's mother watched her husband's progress around the table, and her face couldn't hide the pride that she had for him and his new hobby. Tamara wondered how long they'd been married. The push and pull of their personalities and the quiet love between them spoke to a long life together. Their long marriage reminded her of her parents' thirtieth anniversary party years ago and how madly in love they had been. Tamara was grateful that they had had the chance to celebrate such a milestone before her father had died.

She lifted her gaze from the plate to find Grant staring at her. He didn't shift his gaze at being caught. His unabashed scrutiny unnerved her.

"Tamara, when did you meet Grant? Because imagine my surprise when Martina sprung the news that her son and my daughter were dating."

"We didn't start out dating." Tamara hated being called to the carpet in such a public manner.

"She blew into my world with a business proposition," Grant clarified.

"Trust my daughter to approach things in a business-only style." Her mother turned her attention to Mrs. Benson. "Sorry, Martina."

"Leave these young people to themselves," Mr. Benson interjected. "They certainly don't need any of us to throw in our two cents."

Tamara resisted the urge to stand and give Mr. Benson a high five.

"Grant, why didn't you ever bring her around to meet

me?" Martina looked at Tamara and awarded her with a smile. "I can tell that she has worked to make her parents proud. And she's so mannerly that I'm envious I didn't raise a son who would have the manners to introduce his girlfriend to his family." She turned a stern look at him.

"Well...I—"

"Martina, I'm not going to let my daughter off the hook, either. She didn't trust me to say that she'd met a decent guy. I don't know what has gotten into these young people. They forget how they were raised as soon as they leave the house."

"Ladies, ladies, if you keep up your interrogation, you won't enjoy my food," Mr. Benson said. "If this recipe works, I'm submitting it to the contest."

"Your father fancies himself a chef in the making. The grand prize in this contest he wants to enter is a six-month cooking show. Can you imagine that?"

"I plan to win. If I do, your mother can be my kitchen helper."

Tamara couldn't contain the chuckle that erupted from her. Mrs. Benson cut her eyes at her, then tilted up her nose like the queen she seemed to want to be.

Somehow the tone of the evening finally relaxed. They were all chatting, sharing stories among themselves and telling jokes. Eventually the conversation petered out. Between Grant and her, they had answered so many questions. Too soon the evening ended, and Tamara walked her mother to her car.

"When are you coming for Sunday dinner?" Tamara's mother asked. "And you should come to church with me."

"Good night, Mom. I'll try."

"Heard that before. And I still want to know more about your young man. Not that glossed-over nonsense you fed them. You're treating me as if I'm the stranger."

"Not now, Mom. I just don't know if I want to pursue anything."

Her mother nodded. Her gaze drifted over Tamara's shoulder. She motioned with a push of her chin. "Your young man is waiting for you."

"He's not my young man."

"Maybe you should tell him that. I still can recognize that love-struck look on a man's face." Her mother got in her car, waved to her and drove away.

Tamara turned and walked to where Grant stood with legs apart, hands shoved in pockets, studying her. The night could be over or just beginning. No matter what he wore, no matter under what light he stood, Grant was gorgeous. The man had been blessed with good genes.

"Thanks for introducing me to your mother."

"Likewise," he replied.

"Wasn't as painful as I thought it would be."

"I'm glad my parents met you."

"Your mom scares me, but your dad is a sweetheart."

Grant laughed and then pulled her against his chest. They stood holding each other, swaying without any music.

Tamara sighed. What to do next? Her past told her to back away and run. Her present told her to stay put, hold on. The future scared her the most. She couldn't see beyond the horizon.

Chapter 12

Grant suffered through the film production, which lasted an additional three long days. In order to get over the interruption into his daily life, he had to remind himself that there were many benefits. With one notable exception: Tamara was keeping him at a football-stadium-sized distance.

It was one week after the ambush at his parents' home, and she seemed frozen. Even his calls weren't being returned. Maybe he should be glad that she'd backed off. If he continued down this path, he'd lose his mind. He had to stay away from his vice and regain balance.

At least turning his attention to the latest work in progress kept him busy. The production of the angels and demons game continued to unfold as planned. A few more tweaks and they could move ahead to the next phase. The simultaneous launch of a new game-design software particularly excited him. The software would allow the game to be played on additional platforms. Only a small number of staff knew about this rollout.

"The DBSK creators—Jax and Danny—are here, along with Norton and Hadfield," his assistant informed him.

"Show them in."

"Good to see all of you," he greeted the team as they walked in.

"I hope you liked the latest mock-up," Deetz Norton spoke first.

Grant nodded. "The third spec for the angels looked so real." He laughed. "Well, as real as we think angels look."

"Ever seen an angel?" Deetz asked.

Grant didn't respond. His religious views and thoughts were his own. He wondered where this conversation was going.

"Nah," Hadfield piped up.

"Not me," Jax replied.

"I have," Deetz volunteered. "And no, it wasn't a winged man. Just that I was in a tight spot in my life, faced with a life-and-death situation, and a man appeared to help me. Then when I turned to thank him, he wasn't there. And I would have known if he'd walked away."

"I think that regular people can act like angels. They come into your life to help and then move on," Roy offered.

Grant didn't need any heavy conversation right now.

He'd much rather discuss the project and leave personal testimonies to remain just that, personal.

"Back to the software program that I referred to in the email." Grant redirected their attention. "I met with a graphic illustrator whose work is fantastic and isn't like anything that I've seen." He pulled up the software on his laptop and projected the image on a drop-down screen.

The 3-D images of models for angels and demons flashed onto the screen. Details of the anatomy were unbelievably realistic to capture the roles, tasks and special powers of the characters. Along with the illustration, the color palette added strength to the samples with a bold, heavy outline and vivid shading to make the image pop. They would need to get voice actors with the perfect timbre. But this demo was a must-have.

"Anything that good must cost a bundle," Roy said.

"Expensive, but I'm willing to absorb the cost. There's no way that this won't be a hit," Grant said, confident all the way to his soul in the software program.

"Plus we have the target group for testing," Deetz noted.

"Yep," Roy replied. "I have that already lined up with the interns. I think we should provide teasers to stir the interest and build up for the launch."

Grant shook his head. "I want this group to have the game without any preempt."

"Then maybe at the marketing level," Deetz pushed.

"That will be another project. And we'll go big or go home with the marketing." Grant didn't need this team to stop its focus on fine-tuning the game.

Hadfield pulled out his file to provide his update.

Grant waved him on to begin the detailed report. He admired the leadership skills that Hadfield exhibited. His talent definitely warranted not only nurturing but also the freedom to develop. There was no way that he would let Hadfield get nabbed by another company. He solicited the best or those with potential, and he expected and wanted his staff to stay with the company. The two game designers, Jax and Danny, were also impressive. At the end of this project, he was prepared to offer them full-time employment. Their partnership and ideas could set a new course for Benson Technologies.

Grant remained behind his desk long after the team had left. His imagination still whirred along as if on its own power surge. At some point, he had to stop and let the first edition go to production. As soon as the first edition hit, the new upgrade would already be in the final stages for its launch.

He stretched his limbs. For several hours, he hadn't moved. Time for him to head home. Alone.

Fatigue hit him with a nagging headache. By the time he got home, he wanted only his bed. Food wasn't even an option. After a quick shower, he fell diagonally across the bed, still thinking about the new computer game. He'd have to change the name, but he'd let the marketing team deal with that headache.

Exhaustion smothered him like a warm, heavy blanket. Had he ever seen an angel? He yawned and turned on his side, ready to drift to sleep. Of course he saw an angel. No one could convince him otherwise. His life might have veered so far from the path he took that he might have been in an orange jumpsuit with numbers printed on his chest for his ID. He'd been handed his second chance, and he didn't plan to waste any part of it.

Tamara ended her Monday-morning staff meeting. One day-care helper had called in sick. Mitzy had arrived late. Becky was still in Florida. The mood in the meeting matched the staff's lethargy. Maybe they were all overworked. But theirs wasn't the kind of business that could close its doors for a quick minute.

She missed Becky's ready input. Tamara picked up the phone and dialed.

"What's the word, Becky?" Tamara didn't like that she was having to track down her friend.

"Things got hectic here. Sorry for not giving you an update."

Tamara waited for the dreaded words—*I'm leaving*—that she expected to hear from her friend.

"I'll be back to work by Monday. My mom is much better."

"Yes! And G-Dragon?"

"He's heading off on tour. I only got to see him once. The rest of the time was spent online catching up and talking about ourselves. Not quite the same. And I don't want to be another fan girl hanging out backstage."

"Sorry to hear that," Tamara said. "I'll have a great welcome-home party when you get back."

"I'll hold you to that." They shared a laugh. "So fill me in on the documentary."

"I'm actually looking at an edited piece right now. We made a couple of versions, just in case he didn't care for one thing or the other."

"Sounds like you've worked hard on this."

"I wish that I could take the credit. But the crew did a fantastic job. I'm also thinking of a new program for the academy—we could invite some well-known folks to hold master's-level classes on various subjects, but of course, geared toward our guys." Tamara tossed out the idea to vet with Becky.

"Another major project—sounds exciting."

"Yeah, but we have to make sure it will have great results, too. The big thing will be to get really good people."

"I'd love to run with the master's class project," Becky offered.

"And I'd love to turn this over to you." Tamara picked up on Becky's desire to be back in the office working around people she knew.

Tamara finished up the call. She was thrilled to hear from Becky and to learn that she and G-Dragon had decided to go their separate ways. Love wouldn't elude Becky for long. She only hoped that her friend didn't settle for another frisky singer-celebrity who only wanted to get in her pants.

Her cell phone rang, and she saw it was from Grant's office. This was a change. He'd been calling her in the evening. Now he was calling her in the morning, too.

Not taking his calls was difficult, but she knew she had to wean herself off him. If she kept herself busy, she thought of him only during waking hours. By the time she slept, she was too exhausted to remember any dreams.

She wasn't worried about missing any important up-dates on the documentary. He could go through her assistant for business-related matters. The call went to voice mail. She pressed the icon to play the message.

"Tamara, this is Deanna Rushgrove in the human resources department at Benson Technologies. I think there may be a problem. Your interns didn't show up today for work. And I just got a call from Bill Stevenson that due to altercations among some of the guys, a few will no longer be participating in the program."

"Tamara, Mr. Stevenson is on the phone."

"Put him through." Tamara couldn't believe what she was hearing. "Mr. Stevenson, what on earth is going on?"

"A major fight broke out among the guys. And you know we have a zero-tolerance policy for fighting. Three guys have been expelled from the program and a hearing is scheduled to determine if they will remain at Miller-Brown."

"There must have been a good reason." Tamara would grasp at any straws to save her students. "They had been doing so well. Grant said they are all learning quickly. When they came in they were looking wild, lacked discipline and complained a lot. Now that they have incentives from Grant, they've been working as a team." She realized that she was rambling and forced herself to remain silent.

"Doesn't matter. I just wanted to let you know. I called Mr. Benson to make him aware of the situation. Tomorrow the rest of the group can return. I'm as disappointed as you are, Miss Wendell."

Tamara had known that every day was a tightrope walk with the guys. Emotions, egos and simple teenage hormones could get them in trouble in the blink of an eye. She said good-bye and hung up with Mr. Stevenson, then tossed aside the pen that she had been using to scribble notes and dropped her head into her hands.

"What are you going to do?" she asked herself out loud.

Tamara looked at a framed photo of the guys on their first day at work. No way was she giving up.

"Mitzy, can you get Greta to step in for me? I'll need the afternoon sessions covered. I've got a plan, but I have no idea how long it may take for me to get what I want."

Mitzy chuckled. "They don't know who they are messing with."

"I promise to play nice."

"Good luck."

"I'll need it." She grabbed her car keys and headed out the door.

On the way to Benson Technologies, she placed the necessary call to Grant. She couldn't do this without his help. Hopefully, he'd want to help, although she had been dodging any contact with him for several days. No time to think of any backlash from Grant. Her students needed his help.

These guys had so much potential. One good thing about the fight was that it hadn't happened on the company's grounds. But the liability of having wayward youth among the staff must give HR nightmares. She didn't want their doubts about this program to resurface.

While she needed Grant to help her with her plan to get the guys back into the program, Tamara first needed to know that he still believed in the program. Her decision to not speak to him and put distance between them couldn't have happened at a worse time. She took a deep breath when she pulled up at Benson Technologies and saw that Grant was already waiting for her.

Tamara looked around the parking lot. "You know it might not be safe to stand around like that?"

"Expect someone to kidnap me?" Grant scoffed.

Tamara nodded. "Or carjack." The man couldn't seem to get it through his head that he couldn't go around unaware of his surroundings. She'd also rather scold him than deal with her other overwhelming emotions, which felt like just a constant loop of intensity and vulnerability.

As usual, Grant looked beyond fine. She knew what lay beneath the polo shirt that hung loosely over his khaki pants. Those hands, with long tapered fingers, had once stroked her skin like soft velvet, enticing her to an array of delicious, sensual pleasures.

"The day that I can't walk around and do what I want, then that's the day to pack it all in. I'm a no-fuss, no-frills kind of man."

"Well, someone down-to-earth is always appreciated."

"People don't give a darn about me. They care about the product—that's a good thing. I'm not complaining."

"You're selling yourself short. I know ten guys who already hold you up as their role model."

"They shouldn't."

"That sounds ominous," she responded.

Seconds ticked as the silence surrounded them. There was something that he was hiding. She'd felt it before and dismissed it, but she wouldn't let it go this time.

"Tell me what happened," Tamara said. She knew that he could retreat and shut her out, but she had to try.

Grant sucked in his breath through clenched teeth. His jaw worked as indecision warred quite visibly on his face.

She lost sight of his face when he turned to face the car window. Nothing about his shoulders was relaxed. The longer he remained silent, the more alarmed she got that his secret had enough power to erect a defensive wall against anyone, including her.

"Let's just get to the home," he said at last.

Not quite what she wanted to hear. He joined her in her car and they sped off to their destination. There was no time to coax any information from him.

She pulled in the parking lot of Miller-Brown and switched off the engine. "What's our plan?"

"To get these guys—all of them—back at Benson Technologies." Grant looked at her. "Ready to sway some minds?"

"Always."

He laughed.

Tamara wanted this to work more than anything she'd ever wanted. She kept her reasons close to her heart, knowing that her secrecy with Grant was a bit hypocritical. But he didn't need to know her turmoil. All he needed to know was that she had the best of intentions.

They were granted immediate access to the director's office. Tamara and Grant took their seats to face Mr. Stevenson, who looked ready to battle them.

Although they hadn't devised a specific game plan, Tamara opted to play sidekick and allow Grant to use his quiet but firm nature to take hold. But if that didn't work, she wasn't beyond using tears and full-out begging to get what she wanted.

Grant saw the subtle shift in Tamara's posture as she slid back in the chair. Her gaze shifted from him to Stevenson, clearly giving him the go-ahead to proceed.

"Mr. Stevenson, first, let me say thank you for allowing the guys to participate in this program. I wasn't a keen supporter when Tamara came to me."

"I had to get creative to get him to listen," Tamara interjected.

They all shared a short laugh.

Grant proceeded. "But I did change my mind. And I'm glad that I did."

"Mr. Benson, let me stop you for a second." Stevenson held up his hand. "I am in charge of kids with a wide range of social dysfunctions. I can't have a facility where rules cover one child and not another."

"But what you do with this out-program is also unique and has been running well for almost a year. It's a learning process for all of us, especially the kids," Tamara piped in.

Grant took the relay baton, and added, "I can vouch for the change that I've seen in this group. Within weeks, they have shown a level of maturity and responsibility that makes me proud."

He observed the firm set of Stevenson's mouth. But he also sensed Tamara's panic beginning to grow. She looked at him, silently passing on her message for him to do something.

"Let's not go back and forth. May I see them?" Grant asked.

Stevenson looked surprised. Good. Grant had no idea what he was going to say or do. It was important to stay one step ahead of the director so he couldn't anticipate their argument.

Grant felt his heart pounding as he followed the director down a hallway that opened to several rooms, including larger conference rooms. He was still operating from gut instinct. He hoped that his inner voice continued leading him in the right direction.

He would do whatever was necessary to talk to them, get through to them, in order for them to regain the trust of the director. How far would he go? However far he needed to get them back.

He felt Tamara at his shoulder. A part of him wanted to pull away from her before she could pull away from him again. But that would be an issue for later.

The guys walked into the room, single file and solemn. They stood close together, ten strong. They glanced at him, but no one held eye contact for long. He sensed that Tamara was ready to fidget at his side. He hoped she'd read his body language to stay calm.

Grant took a deep breath. Time to channel his father from back in the days of his own youthful rebellion. He'd see that vein pop in the middle of his father's forehead and know that he was in deep, deep trouble. He hoped the director would let him scare the boys straight.

Every group had a leader, whether they picked one or one naturally emerged. Frederick, the tallest and eldest, had that honor. Each group also had the "baby" of the group, the one who brought out the protective nature of the alphas. Graham was this group's "baby" since he had a tiny stature and was known for being mouthy.

"What happened?" Grant barked out the question. Just to be sure that they understood, he pinned Frederick with a hard, cold look.

The young man stepped forward. His mouth was tight, chin jutted forward. No remorse was visible.

"Cut the attitude, kid," Stevenson warned.

Youthful rebellion was in full swing, as Frederick didn't change his attitude one bit.

Grant snapped his fingers to get back his attention. "I'm waiting. What happened?"

"Since we started at Benson Technologies, guys in here at the home have been giving us grief. We expected that. No biggie." He emphasized with a flick of his hand. "Then this newbie comes in and tries to get respect from everyone else by messing with us. Plus he's one of them rich boys gone bad. He thinks that he should have been picked for the internship."

Grant didn't need a crystal ball to know this scenario was a powder keg.

"Every day, he pecked like a hen at us. Then he started jostling, bumping shoulders."

"Did you tell anyone?" Tamara asked, with a hopeful lilt.

But Grant knew that answer, too.

Sure enough, Frederick shook his head.

"Why?" Tamara's voice raised a pitch.

Grant wanted to probe further, but he held back, allowing her the floor. She'd brought him in to help, not to take over.

Frederick responded, thumping his chest. "In here, we take care of each other."

"No, I do that," Mr. Stevenson corrected.

Their collective response to the director's declaration was clear. They hunched their shoulders and tuned out.

Tamara grumbled, removing herself to one side.

Grant motioned with his hand to continue.

"We can handle it." Frederick swung around and the arc of his arm encompassed most of the guys, except the last three. "But rich boy and his boys did a divide-and-conquer move that night on those three— the youngest. Some guys came and told the rest of us what happened. We had to take care of business, that night or some other night."

"Busted noses, cracked ribs, black eyes." The director listed the injuries.

Grant eyed the three who were expelled. A few black-and-blue marks, but otherwise they seemed to have come out of the fight to the advantage.

"Didn't you realize that once you threw a punch, you were done with the program?" Tamara asked the question to which they all knew the answer.

Frederick nodded. "We live here. Going to work is like a breath of fresh air. It's what we hope we can do when we're on our own and out of the system without the curfew and rules. Until then, at the end of the day, we're here. Night after night, we get tested by those who don't care about your program." He pointed to Tamara. "Don't care about the rules." He pointed to Stevenson. "Don't care if someone wants to give a second chance." He looked straight at Grant. "Some days I can brush it off. I'm the oldest. I made my mistakes and yet, Miss

Tamara didn't think that I was too old to save." He tilted his head toward Grant. "And you told us about your demons and how you came through. So, we are listening."

If Tamara's gaze could touch him, Grant imagined it would burn right through him. Maybe it was best that everything had come out on the table. Another milestone to be experienced with Tamara.

"Mr. Stevenson, is there any way that if I vouch for them and the work they've done for the company that we can make an exception?" Grant refused to surrender to the director's decision.

"I will vouch for them, too," Tamara spoke softly.

"We have a committee who makes these rules. They are not policies that have no meaning. These are the same kids that the schools, the community, the public want punished."

"I understand, Director." Grant dragged his hand over his head. He struggled to keep his frustration under wraps. "I'm not saying that rules shouldn't be upheld. I can't justify what they did. I can only tell you that, as someone who was once standing where they stand, I would want someone to fight on my behalf and to keep on fighting."

The silence hovered, heavy, poignant and full of questions.

"I had everything but still wanted more. I wanted respect. Computer nerd wasn't a label that I embraced, even if it matched me exactly. So I joined up with a street gang."

Grant heard Tamara's soft *no* of disbelief.

"The group didn't operate overtly like a gang. Instead, they just seemed like some guys who were all about leadership activities and mentoring. It was a regular band of brothers.

"First we hung out, going to movies, hanging out at parties, playing video games. Then some older guys got involved and took over. Suddenly we were doing what they suggested, and they were calling all the shots.

"It started small with petty crimes. Then they introduced some of the willing guys to stealing cars. One day I was picked up at my house by one of the guys. We were going over to another guy's house for a party. Don't know what triggered the cops to check the car, but we got pulled over.

"Instead of pulling over, the driver hit the gas and we took off. I can't begin to tell you what I felt for fifteen minutes of a high-speed chase. Then we clipped a car and went flipping over and over. The driver was thrown from the car. I was anchored in by my seat belt, but I injured my neck and lost feeling in my legs for months.

"Short story—the car was stolen. Drugs in the trunk. My father was this close to letting me suffer through jail and take my chances." He held up his thumb and index finger to emphasize the slim chance.

"My mother stepped up and got a good lawyer. Proved that I had no intention to do anything because I expected to be back within minutes. I had a scheduled tutoring session, which was the only thing that saved my butt with the law…but not with my father."

His angel, an elderly woman with a kind face and gentle voice whom he'd never seen before, had arrived on the scene that horrendous night. She'd stooped low to the wreckage of the car and stayed at his side, holding his bloody hand, comforting him until the ambulance and police had arrived. He'd asked about her when the paramedics came, but they said no one had been there. Plus, they'd had to pry open the door, so no one could have been at his side, much less holding his hand. But he didn't care what they'd said. He knew what he'd heard and seen. From that day on, he'd turned around his life.

"Guys, do you want to continue?" Grant asked.

"Yes." Their voices echoed in a chorus.

"Can you swear that you will allow the administration to intervene before you make a move against another kid?" The boys all nodded. Grant turned to the director. He wanted to gauge if there was any change, any softening up, that could work in his favor with Stevenson.

Tamara stepped closer to him. Her arm brushed against his and then came to rest on it. He resisted every urge not to seek the warmth of her hand. He wanted to slip his palm against hers and intertwine their fingers.

It meant so much to him that she hadn't shunned him after his revelation.

"Boys, Mr. Benson, Miss Wendell, I will request of the committee that they reverse the decision…this time. I hope that I don't come to regret this."

Chapter 13

"Pizza is served." Grant brought a large pie covered with colorful vegetables and pepperoni onto his backyard deck.

"Smells delicious." Tamara held out her plate as he served her two slices. "You're spoiling me." She waited until he was seated next to her with his slice of pizza. "You know, this view is marvelous."

"As if the view from your penthouse isn't," Grant teased. "Plus I think the company is better than the view."

"Maybe." She made a face at him. "With Becky back in town and a bit sad that she didn't run off with her hip hop star, I'm homeless for the night. Wanted to give her some space to mourn. I'm not her favorite BFF at the moment."

Grant softly rubbed her cheek. "Not too many things worse than a heartbreak."

"Depends. I've got regrets that hurt as badly as a heartbreak."

Grant observed the sadness on Tamara's face that always seemed to be just below the surface.

"You've got a great bunch of kids. And you've got me."

"You've got your company. You've got me," she responded.

"So we *are* on the same page." Grant offered the reminder more for himself than her. These quiet moments where they sat together, enjoying beer and pizza, had a domestic feel to them. He'd never pictured himself as one to settle down, especially after his engagement to Vanessa. But spending time with Tamara and chatting about their future raised his hope.

Tamara saluted him. "Yes, General Benson. You're building an empire. I'm just trying to raise a few more empire builders." She turned toward him. Their lounge chairs sat side by side. "I'm still on the same page. We're still no strings attached."

The statement nestled in the foundation of their relationship. Despite the rules, he found that he wanted to kick the stipulation out of view. But Tamara had been adamant. He'd tried to convince himself that he could play along, that he could be as pragmatic as her.

Grant nuzzled her cheek before giving her a peck.

"You know I don't want you for your money, babe," Tamara said.

"What about my trade secrets?"

"Nope. Not that either."

Grant played with her fingers, intertwining his with hers so they were clasped together.

"It's what you do with your hands." She kissed the back of his hand. "It's what you do with your mouth." She leaned over and planted a kiss on his mouth. "And the rest...I'll let you know later." She leaned back in the chair and surveyed him with a small smile.

They finished the pizza, enjoying the comfortable temperature as twilight settled around them. Fireflies zipped around the backyard. Soft strains of a piano being played over the outdoor sound system drifted through the evening. Grant sighed, relaxing into the chair.

"Earlier, you opened up about your teenage years," Tamara said.

He closed his eyes. Waiting. Dreading.

"I appreciated what you said. I know it must've been tough, maybe not with the kids, but with Stevenson and me. Just want to say that I'm proud of you."

Grant opened his eyes. The dread evaporated and blew away. He'd never cared what another woman thought of him until Tamara came with her killer golf swing into his life. Now a sense of relief washed over him.

He offered, "I hadn't planned on unveiling my past. But I'd sacrifice my privacy for those guys anytime. They are at the critical place that I once was."

Grant gently cupped Tamara's face between his hands, kissing her softly, willing her not to ever change her feelings toward him. "Let's head upstairs."

* * *

Tamara followed Grant to his bedroom. Just watching him climb the stairs was a turn-on. By the time they entered his room, she couldn't wait to get her hands on him. He also had the same idea, as he playfully groped her body.

She didn't need a man with exotic eyes of hazel or green to capture her interest. Not at all. Grant's solid, dark brown eyes framed with thick black lashes could be just as heart fluttering.

As for his mouth, small or wide didn't matter. She loved his lips that had a luscious softness and fullness, with the perfect Cupid's bow shape that framed his beautiful smile. After all, lips weren't meant only to be watched and admired. They deserved to be sampled and tested for their power. As she pulled him closer, the pair of full lips she'd been watching partially opened with a slight upward curve and a delicious inviting quality. She locked lips with him, starting their dance of passion.

She slid her hands up his back. Her fingers splayed over the ripples of the muscles along his shoulder blades. His heart beat heavily against her ear.

"Do you trust me?" she asked, her voice muffled as her lips brushed his chest. "Do you trust me?" she repeated.

"Yes," he hissed.

"I want to be your girlfriend."

"Okay." His wariness seemed to drag the word beyond its two syllables.

She didn't want to go back to the way things were. Yet, the next level had a scary thrill that made her want to proceed with caution.

She pointed to his chest. "One day, I want in. I'll wait."

Before he could respond, she kissed him. She didn't want to hear his response at that moment.

She stood on her tiptoes to meet his mouth again. Grant picked her up and carried her to the bed. Her arms locked around his neck; her body pressed against his chest. She kissed his jaw, loving the straight line and strong angle of his profile. Another kiss touched the corner of his mouth. His mouth twitched and a sigh escaped.

Tamara closed her eyes. Inside his arms, the world seemed far away. Nothing to intrude on their moment.

He lifted her chin with the crook of his finger. "Show me those beautiful eyes."

When she complied, he continued, "I may not be the most open person about my heart. But I speak from in here." He pointed to his chest. "Tamara, I love you, have loved you, and will always love you. What we have is special and unique, as it should be between soul mates."

Tamara bit her lip to keep the tears away. His romantic declaration meant the world to her, erasing the mounting doubt that had been overwhelming her.

His gaze consumed her, sweeping her up into a fiery blaze. Then he looked down at her mouth and kissed her ever so gently. She closed her eyes, letting her other senses take over.

His mouth closed in, hovered, his ragged breaths soothing her. His firm lips pressed gently and she opened up. He slid his tongue in, and her moans sounded so far away.

Her mouth laid out the welcome mat, inviting and

coaxing him deeper in. Her hands staked their claim to his chest. He cradled the back of her head, his fingers intertwined with her hair.

Their bodies pressed together, sending their sexual thermometer through the roof. She felt his arousal, hard and at full length, against her pelvis. Sheer pleasure and delicious, sinful thrill shot through her entire being.

"Let's not land. Let's not ever come down," she whispered.

"Suspended animation—a bit unreal." He chuckled near her ear.

"All of this is unreal."

"Then let's do something that is real and leaves no doubt what this is." He undressed her, tossing her clothing to the side. Every time his fingers touched her skin, she shivered in delight.

She rubbed his shaft, sliding her hands down his aroused length. "Let me play with you, baby. Give me all the time I need to touch you here and here and here." Her thumb slid over his head. He had to grab her wrist a couple of times to slow or stop completely. From the veins along his neck, she was sure that his self-control couldn't be guaranteed.

Grant protected with a condom. His legs shook as her hands slid up along his inner thighs. His stroke started hard and fast. She loved the intensity, urging him with her pelvis to keep that pace. Hard and fast worked. Hard and rough satisfied. "Are we going to do this all night long?" Her words hitched every time he drove in.

"Yep. All night long."

"Music to my ears."

* * *

As the launch date approached, Grant had to cancel on coming to several home-cooked dinners. His mood was dark and brooding and his mind easily distracted over the latest glitch in the game. Tamara tried to take it all in stride. After all, they were a couple in love.

Now, three weeks without seeing Grant had put Tamara in a foul mood. The academy used to be on her mind every waking hour, until she'd met Grant. She'd carved out time to spend with him to the point that it was now part of her routine. She couldn't believe how dependent she had become on seeing him. After the latest cancellation, however, she had agreed to come home early from work to eat a concoction that Becky had cooked, and she hoped it would take her mind off Grant.

She entered the apartment and almost ran back into the hallway. "What the heck is that smell?"

Becky popped her head out of the kitchen. With a big smile, she said, *"Annyeonghaseyo."* Then she bowed and headed back to the kitchen "It's Korean cuisine tonight."

"And we're eating whatever is smelling up the entire house?"

"That's *kimchi*—pickled cabbage."

"That's our dinner?" Tamara headed for the refrigerator door. "Where's the number for pizza?"

"Oh, stop being a brat." Becky pushed her away from the fridge. "Go wash up and then come back. The rice is almost done. I'll barbecue strips of beef in a few."

Tamara complied but had to ask as she headed into her room, "Why are we eating Korean food? Why are you dressed up and wearing makeup?" Becky did have a history of coming up with good recipes. In a pinch, she always had a quick, tasty meal tucked in that crazy brain. This, however, was not her usual M.O.

"I want to send a video to G-Dragon of what I've done. You never know, it could be the selling point between me and another homegirl."

"That's the craziest thing I've heard from you. Since I know you're not kidding, let me be clear. You're not filming me." Tamara undressed and changed into her sweats and a T-shirt. She'd wait to take a shower until after she'd eaten the strongly scented meal. Despite her misgivings, though, her stomach growled as other enticing smells suffused the air.

The intercom buzzed, signaling a visitor.

"Oh, by the way, I invited a few folks."

"Really?" Tamara groaned. She didn't feel up to company. Becky had such an assortment of friends she collected that Tamara wasn't sure who would be walking through the door.

Since the guests started to arrive, Tamara headed back to her bedroom. She was going quite casual, but changed into jeans and a blouse.

"Tamara, what's taking you so long?" Becky stood in her doorway, motioning her to come.

"What's the rush? This is your gig."

"People brought friends. It's kind of crowded." Becky wrung her hands. The perky, easygoing Becky had fled.

Tamara hurried with her dressing and headed out. She stopped short at her bedroom door, and then she decided to pull it closed. When she'd left to get dressed, two guests had been there. Now the room had about fifteen people, and the whole party looked like a poster for the United Nations. As she surveyed the room, she realized she didn't know anyone. Nothing new. Becky, the social beacon, had attracted the usual partygoers.

Becky clapped her hands. "Hey, could you not put your feet on my couch?"

Tamara had a feeling this dinner party was going to be short-lived. "Light up that cigarette in here and I will shove it down your throat," she said to the man standing next to her.

The offender hurriedly slipped the cigarette back in his pocket and avoided eye contact.

Tamara continued into the kitchen, where it looked as if a bomb had exploded. "Where's the food?" Tamara opened the oven and then the refrigerator.

"I kind of lost my appetite to cook after I saw all those people. I'd only bought enough ingredients for a small dinner party. People asked if they could bring a friend—one friend. This is like feeding a village," Becky complained.

Tamara heard the buzzer announcing another visitor's arrival. "So what are we eating?" Her stomach grumbled, a perfect match with her mood.

"I ordered the Korean food, instead. This might be the delivery guy."

Sure enough, the delivery guy arrived with a wide array of Korean cuisine. Tamara pulled out various platters for the food setup. She was willing to do that much. Once the food had been laid out on the dining table, the crowd moved in like locusts and demolished it with an energy and efficiency that was frightening.

"Who are some of these people?"

"Some are from the language class that I take in

the evening. Some are from my aerobics class." Becky pointed to a few heads.

"From the looks of things, that weight management plan might need to be rechecked."

Becky elbowed her to hush. "A few are from the academy. Contacts that I've made. Figured it was important to keep them in the loop."

"Cool idea, but maybe they didn't need to meet under *our* roof."

"Hey, Becky," said a woman who was walking in their direction. "I heard that you're working with Grant Benson. Lucky you. Heard you said he was fantastic and gorgeous. Care to share?"

Tamara's eyebrows perked as she awaited Becky's response. A smile tugged at her mouth as she enjoyed her roommate's embarrassment.

"Think you could get me a job?" the woman said. She stood in front of them, looking like a million dollars. Her dark hair shone with healthy vibrancy. Her features had an exotic appeal, as if she was a blend of many ethnicities. She was beautiful and she knew it.

"I—I—I don't have those connections." Tamara's glare caused Becky to stammer.

"Oh, I bet you do. You and your roommate."

She stopped and crossed her arms. "What I want to know is, what is the mastermind working on? Word is that there's a new game system that's supposed to kick the other game systems to the curb."

"What do you want?" Becky asked, bristling.

"Information." The woman smiled. A million dollar smile. "I can make it worth your while."

"Who are you?" Tamara didn't care if this was Becky's friend or associate.

"Isabelle Vandusen, a reporter."

Becky snorted. "You don't look like a reporter. You look like a high-priced witch."

"Child, step back." Isabelle said. She turned her attention to Tamara. "You look sensible enough. You run the academy of teens who work for Benson. Mind if I chat with them?"

"You don't go near them." Tamara seethed at the woman's boldness.

"Objection duly noted. I wanted to put you on notice." She sashayed past them. "Ladies, have a good evening. Next time that you want to throw a decent party, get in touch."

Tamara sealed Isabelle Vandusen to her memory. She seriously doubted that the woman was a reporter. Maybe she was one of those gold diggers who had made Grant's life hellish. The woman had a cold, calculating look that made her seem like an opportunist. Just as Vanessa had had when they'd come face-to-face at the basketball game. The question was whether Grant found that type attractive. Did she have to sharpen her skills to compete? It had never been her style to fight over a man. She busied herself with another lettuce wrap of beef *bulgogi* and shoved it into her mouth.

Life seemed to be chugging along happily for Tamara. The guys' internship continued without any further hitches. She'd been invited back to Grant's parents' for dinner in a few days, an event that she looked forward to. Her mother had taken up scrapbooking as a hobby, which now often took her down memory lane. Even Becky had taken on new hobbies, particularly anything that fell under the Korean culture umbrella.

In a month, the internship would be over. The guys would be faced with changes such as finishing up at the academy, heading back into the world and searching for jobs. They were all due to receive glowing reports from the supervisors at Benson Technologies, so recommendations wouldn't be difficult to get for the job-hunting process.

No matter how much advance planning was done, the transition always was an emotional wallop for the youth. The academy would get them involved in planning their own graduation celebration. In the meantime, they had to jump the hurdle and prepare for the unexpected.

With Becky's tenacity, the academy had recruited seasoned workers and high-level professionals to talk about job hunting in that particular economy, and they would cover everything from creating the résumé, interviewing and learning about the basic clothing must-haves. Her mother had also volunteered. As a former English professor, she worked on the guys' diction and grammar. Thankfully she had the patience to survive the guys' minimeltdowns as they tried to remember the parts of speech.

Tamara spent an hour catching up on correspondence and making her to-do list for the upcoming week.

Pretty soon it was time to close up the academy for the weekend. A few of the guys popped their heads in to say hi. She heard the shuttle pull off to take them back to the boys' home. She wished she could avoid the mountain of paperwork and drive off for a quick break. Instead, she opted to stick around a little longer and tackle the stockpile.

Slowly, she managed to make headway. This would be one more long night spent alone, without Grant. He had come to the final part of his new-game project and the fine details consumed his entire day. The level of security around the product would rival that of any government top-secret project. Every aspect was under wraps. Whenever she managed to talk to him, he was so preoccupied that their conversation would peter into silence. She missed him so much and sometimes resented how much his company took over his time. Closing her eyes, she could almost conjure his scent, his touch and the deep timbre of his voice.

"Hey, sweetheart, got a minute?"

"Yeah, Mom, come in. I thought you'd left."

"Everything A-okay on the home front?"

"Yeah." Tamara hadn't expected that question at all.

"Just wondering. You've been looking a bit down. Martina said that Grant was tied up with his new game design. And, well, I thought about you and how you're handling it."

"Some days, I understand that Grant's busy on his project. But some of my guys are graduating from school. Moving on. Even Becky seems to be in love. That's when I get a bit resentful that he's not available to spend more time with me." Tamara couldn't believe that she had to fight back tears. Suddenly expressing what was on her mind made her sad, even wistful.

"Sounds like good news for the people in your life,

sweetheart." Her mother came around the desk and hugged her. "All I heard were blessings."

Tamara had to fight doubly hard to maintain control. She hadn't cried in her mother's lap since junior high when the guy she liked rejected her and then read her diary aloud at school. But it had been a while since she'd opened up about her feelings for her mother's judgment. So her kind, measured response touched Tamara's sentimental nerve. She sniffed back a few loose tears.

"Look, I know how painful life can be, but these changes are wonderful. And I'm one hundred percent sure that Grant is there for you. Don't let the doubts take over your mind or they will war with your soul. Protect that new love, child. Can I just say that it warms my heart to see my daughter so in love?"

Tamara hadn't pinned a name to what she'd felt. Her feelings were like a roller coaster, with sudden highs and lows. Her thoughts about Grant swirled, pushing and pulling her reasoning apart. All she wanted to do was surrender to her heart because it most certainly had been captured and was being held hostage by Grant.

"Honey, before I wait any longer, there's something else I must tell you."

Tamara didn't like the change in her mother's tone, nor the serious, worried expression she had.

"I heard something among the young guys but didn't know if it was worth mentioning."

"What?" Tamara knew her mother was old-fashioned. She was probably going to tell on them for trash-talking or something like that.

"A couple of the guys were approached by a reporter."

"What? When?" Tamara recalled Isabelle Vandusen's bold comments. She'd checked with the guys the day after meeting her, but none of them had heard of her.

Her mother shrugged. "I didn't get the impression that it was that long ago. Maybe yesterday or the day before?"

"Why would a reporter approach them? Because they work with Grant?"

"That's what I thought." Her mother looked thoughtful. "They mentioned that the reporter asked about their internship."

"What did this reporter want to know?"

"She asked about the new game."

"But the guys wouldn't know about that." Tamara tried to think ahead for motive. The guys weren't in Grant's inner circle to know details. Why use them?

Her mother shrugged.

Tamara pushed for more details. "Did they say anything else? Please try to remember."

"Apparently the reporter offered them money. A couple of the older ones had been testing the game in the early stage."

"Did they accept the money?" Tamara offered up a quick prayer, hoping that the guys hadn't done anything unethical.

"I walked closer and they stopped talking."

Tamara stood, inwardly cringing at what had to be done. "I have to tell Grant."

"Maybe you should talk to the boys first. Make sure that they didn't take money or say anything. Try to minimize the damage."

"You're right." Tamara would love to rectify the situation and sweep it under the rug, if at all possible. It was possible that her guys hadn't done anything. But once their integrity came under suspicion, then that cloud would remain over them forever. She knew the disastrous consequences of fear and suspicion. No way would she repeat the same mistake.

Chapter 14

By the time Tamara arrived home, she had contacted Stevenson to let him know she'd be at Miller-Brown early the next morning to talk to the guys. Emails had been sent to all of them, but as expected, the suspected ones didn't respond. Meanwhile, the others tried to distance themselves from the situation by pointing fingers. She didn't go into details, but Stevenson got the gist that the meeting was crucial.

"Will you come with me tomorrow?" Tamara asked Becky after she had revealed her mother's earlier conversation. They sat on the living room floor cross-legged, a mirror image of each other.

"I'll come, but you have to call Grant right away," Becky protested.

"I do plan to tell him. It's not like I didn't mention Isabelle Vandusen to him. No one could find anything on her, if that was even her real name. But this is different."

"How? Because it's kids from the academy? This involves Grant, his company, his work. What is the problem?" Becky shook her head. "This is beyond ridiculous. Why are you sticking your neck out for these kids to this extent? I understand about the fighting, but this is taking it to a whole other level."

"Don't judge before you know all the facts." Tamara didn't need to hear the same message that intruded in her thoughts. "Just don't." Guilt churned in her stomach, always reminding her that she had judged with blind passion. The bigger picture had to be considered, not for her, but for the young men.

"If you don't tell him, I will."

"Why would you do that?"

"Because you're about to destroy what you have with Grant just to prove you don't need him in your life. It's all about your young men being used as the obstacle. And I like Grant. He's a decent guy. You deserve each other, for goodness' sake"

"You've got it wrong." Tamara stood. "I said that I'd take care of it. And those guys are not going to be used as scapegoats by anyone, even you or Grant." Tamara's anger stiffened her spine like steel. "If you don't like it, then we have problem."

The threat hung in the air, locked and loaded.

Becky blinked first. "I just think that you're losing perspective with these boys. You can't save all of them. Your ego is getting in the way of your better judgment."

"I'm going to damn well try. I don't plan to give up on them. And I didn't think you would."

"I have compassion for them. You seem to have an obsession for them."

Tamara hated when Becky spoke to her in that overly calm manner. It only made her angrier. "Some kids need a helping hand. And if we turn our backs on them, they face a bleak future. A generation behind bars will be our legacy."

"Free will. They have to learn to make the right choices. You aren't going to be around for the rest of their lives running behind them with your hands out-stretched in case they fall."

"Maybe by the time I can no longer catch them, someone will have stepped up to take my place in the community of compassion."

Becky exhaled her exasperation. "I don't get it."

"And maybe you won't ever. Here, I thought you would be the eternal optimist."

Silence hung heavy, dark and clinging to everything. They had had minor skirmishes, as most best friends do, but this had the rumblings of a war. Tamara had drawn her line and stood by her convictions.

Becky grabbed her car keys. "I'm heading out."

Becky's criticism had stung. Maybe some distance between them would be best. Tamara bit her lip to stop from calling her back.

"You have one day to tell Grant. Or I'm going to tell him."

"And then you can find a new job."

Becky nodded. "And a new home."

Tamara wanted to press the rewind button. Her fight wasn't with Becky. How could this have gone so far? This wasn't about sabotaging her feelings for Grant, either. No one understood why she was protective of the young men. Her obsession, as Becky accused, was a misnomer. She truly wanted the best for them and was willing to advocate on their behalf with every inch of her being. Trusting that someone else would care about their well-being didn't come easy. This was the first time that her vocation had the potential to rip apart a personal relationship. But once her mother had shone a light on her true feelings, Tamara had felt a new sense of freedom.

The morning scurried along as if on its own mission. Tamara spent the early hours with the guys, asking them about the overheard conversation. Their honesty touched her to the point that she couldn't hold back tears. Vandusen had contacted them, offering money for information. She'd laced her requests with outrageous promises. But not only had they refused her bribes, they'd turned the tables and followed her, taping her meeting with her boss—Vanessa Lord.

Tamara knew she had to get the information to Grant. But now that she'd recovered somewhat from the revelations, she wanted to pay her respects to someone who was always in her heart. She walked through the doors to the mausoleum. The interior was solemn but bright, catering to the surviving loved ones who visited and stayed awhile to search for peace. She took her usual seat in front of the nameplate of the young soul who had brought focus to her life.

DARTH DAWSON

For God has not destined us for wrath, but to obtain salvation through our Lord Jesus Christ, who died for us so that whether we are awake or asleep we might live with him. 1 Thessalonians 5:9-10

1977-2009

"Hi, Tamara," said an older woman as she approached the nameplate.

"Oh, hi, Mrs. Dawson. How are you?" Tamara scooted along the seat to allow Darth's mother enough space to sit.

"I'm doing fine. Here to wish Darth a happy birthday?" The woman's hair had turned almost gray after her son's death. Lines etched her forehead and cheeks.

Tamara nodded. "I wanted him to know that I didn't forget."

"I'm sure he knows, honey. You've been coming here for three years." She placed her hand over Tamara's. "It's time to let go though."

"I can't."

"You must. I know you mean well. Your heart is beautiful. But this isn't your burden to bear."

Tamara blinked back the tears. "I was so sure that I was doing the right thing. We organized and protested against him attending our university. We didn't see him as a person. He was this ex-con with no heart and no feelings. We...I was so wrapped up with righteous indignation..." Tamara wiped away the tears angrily. "What if he had attended our school? He could have gone on to have a life, a family. I wasn't doing what my parents would have done. There was no compassion in my actions—it was all just sheer ego."

Mrs. Dawson held her hand. "Darth made bad choices early in life and paid his debt to society. He tried to get on the right path, but he couldn't seem to outrun his past. So he turned to what was familiar." His mother gave a weary sigh. "And this was the consequence. Nothing that you did." She pushed up Tamara's chin with her finger. "You can't turn back time. I know about all you've done because of my son. I love you for it." She lowered her hand and turned to the place where her son's body resided. "This is one of those times, though, when you have to let go and let God take over."

Tamara listened to everything she said. She'd heard the same admonishment from Becky before. She had to let go.

"Use what you know to inspire those kids in your academy. Teach them to be role models to those that come after them."

"I can do that," Tamara responded. She thought about the reporter and how easily her guys had drawn suspicion. She finally felt ready to head back out into the world and talk to Grant.

"Good." Mrs. Dawson pulled out her Bible. "I'll stay here for a while."

Tamara got home to an empty apartment. As she walked through the large area turning on lights, she missed her best friend's cheery greeting.

She dropped her car keys on the counter. Heck, she'd been missing Becky ever since she'd gotten serious with G-Dragon. Even in the off-again, on-again rhythm of that relationship, Becky dealt with the ups and downs with an ease that she envied.

Becky didn't reach for perfection. She certainly didn't spend all her time looking for the bad stuff. Living a life of blind optimism scared Tamara. But Becky's confidence in life could teach her a lesson or two. She hoped that they could call a truce between them.

She sighed. Whom she really wanted right now was Grant. It was once their hyper-charged sexual encounters that could soothe, satisfy and stir her passion into a frenzy. Now, she wanted more and was willing to make her declaration not only to herself, but to him. She grabbed her keys and headed out.

Driving across town took less time than normal. With quick steps, she hurried to his door.

He opened it before she could knock. He was standing in his pajama bottoms, chest bared.

Tamara didn't say anything. She pushed him into the house, wrapped her arms around him then kicked the door closed with her foot.

Tamara didn't let go. She couldn't let go. Feeling Grant's body, hard and ready, pressed against her frame sent her senses into a spin.

Locked in his embrace, her head against his chest, she closed her eyes as she inhaled his smell.

In an effortless swoop, he lifted her. She looked into his dark eyes, sinking deliciously into their power, as if dipping into warm chocolate.

She could practically taste the sweetness of his kisses ravishing her neck and shoulders.

"I want you right here, right now." His words were muffled with his mouth pressed against the mound of her breast.

"I'd have it no other way." She meant every word.

She wrapped her legs around his waist, strapping in for the ride of her life. Her heart thumped in anticipation. Every part of her cried out for satisfaction. She had no doubt that Grant would pay up—big.

They spun, staggered and bumped against furniture until landing in a soft heap in a plush armchair.

She pinned Grant down, grinding her hips against his, anxious for the barriers of clothing to be gone. Her need for their naked skin to connect was primal.

She took Grant's hand and directed it to her hip. He could have touched any part of her and she would have melted.

She guided his hand from her hip to her abdomen. Instead of calming the jitters, his hand encouraged the frenetic energy to swirl in the pit of her stomach and shoot off into and through each limb.

She inhaled sharply.

He raised up and kissed her abs, creating a hot trail of desire with his soft pecks. Tiny explosions went through her system with each touch of his lips.

Her fingers grabbed the sides of the chair to anchor her. Nothing held her head in place, though. Her neck arched back, pushing up her chest, where his mouth awaited as if ready to pluck her.

A soft swish of his tongue against her nipple caused an involuntary recoil. She slipped her hands around his neck to maintain her balance. Grant's head landed against her breasts. They both moaned from the intensity of the moment.

He was hers and she was his. Every part of her responded to his attention with a heightened sense of anticipation.

Her body craved the chance to elicit a similar reaction from Grant.

His body shone with ripples of muscles across his chest and abdomen. Only a small wisp of hair sat in the middle of his chest, and a thin trail started below his belly button and continued south.

He kissed her neck. She wrapped her leg around his waist, drawing him as close to her body as possible. She unsnapped his pants and pushed them, along with his underwear, past his hips and down his long legs. His shaft stood out rock hard and ready. She gripped his butt cheeks, ready to pleasure him the way he'd done to her so many times.

Chapter 15

"Did you just use me?" Grant asked playfully as he stroked her back.

She nodded. Her head turned to the side. Her eyes were closed, revealing nothing.

But he knew her body so intimately that he knew she was hiding something.

He propped up on his elbow.

"Come on. Talk to me."

"No. I'd like to remember this."

"You say that as if we're never going to do this ever again." He kissed each of her shoulder blades. Her skin was deliciously warm beneath his lips.

Already he was hard and wanted to continue from where they had left off.

"Why are you so kind?" She turned onto her back.

He couldn't help soaking in the sight of her nipples

perked and ready for the tasting…or maybe she was just as aroused as he.

Only one way to find out.

He slid his hand along her body down to her soft mound. His fingers played and discovered the telltale moisture that he was delighted to discover.

Her phone buzzed. He ignored it, continuing with his exploration. She slid away from him, reaching for the phone. Grant frowned. They'd never let anything interrupt their intimate time. Maybe she had to take the call.

"Will you be around later?" she asked, after a brief, cryptic one-sided conversation on the phone.

He nodded, not trying to hide his irritation.

"I've got to take care of something. But I promise that I'll let you know what's up."

Grant gave another terse nod. He felt shut out that she wouldn't or couldn't share whatever was bothering her.

His mother had urged him to trust. In other words, he should allow one hundred percent access to his heart. He remembered her words: *it's what you do when you're in love.*

Grant set down the latest business innovator award given to Benson Technologies on the bookshelf that housed several others. In the company's short history, significant milestones charted its national success. Now he looked forward to making its global footprint, first in Korea, then China and Japan. All the hard work, long hours, and cancelled dinners with Tamara weren't in vain. Even her minidocumentary had been received with positive reviews.

The bad had a way of also galloping headlong at him.

Competitors didn't play nice and they had no problem tripping him up in any way possible.

The new game and game system were scheduled for launch the next day. Wednesday, hump day, seemed like the perfect time to shake up the gaming world. The marketing team and the advertisers had worked around the clock to make it happen. And yet he would be holding his breath until he got the public's reaction. He knew that the guys held his same level of excitement for the game. But only after the gamers gave a thumbs-up would he relax and breathe again.

The time changed on the desk clock. Almost midnight, and he wasn't even close to going home. He rubbed his chin, his fingers scratching the stubble of new growth. His eyes felt heavy and swollen.

His phone rang. His staff knew that he was accessible twenty-four hours, every day of the week. But when his head of product security was calling at this late hour, something was up.

"Grant here."

"Sir, we have a problem."

"I'm in the office. Come on up."

A few minutes later, his head of product security sat across from him. His grim demeanor set the tone that whatever he was about to tell him would not end well. Grant motioned with his hand for him to start.

"I have a source at Trident News Media. They plan to preempt your launch tomorrow with their own report slamming the new product and system."

"That's a pain in the butt, but not detrimental." Competitors always caught the scent of a launch in its final days.

"They are getting the information from a competitor, who is also going to put out a negative report on you."

Grant shrugged. "Annoying, but we'll be fine."

"Since all of this happened fairly quickly, I did a quick sweep of the computers."

Grant nodded. His staff was aware that nothing on their computers was off-limits to security surveillance.

"I'm still working on where the source is. But this problem has crossed departments. In the mix are the interns."

"Come again?" Grant didn't expect that revelation.

"Not all, but definitely a couple have been using the computers to communicate with someone. Nothing definitive, but highly suspect given the language."

Grant took the paperwork that was handed to him. He scanned the report. Disappointment mounted as he saw the names of the guys for whom he'd gone to bat.

The last few pages showed copies of emails. The name on the email exchange pierced through his defenses, precise and deadly.

"The head of the academy is involved."

Grant read the email. Clearly Tamara knew about the breach and was actively covering it up. He could accept her need to protect her students. She'd been protecting them from day one. But what he didn't expect was that she hadn't told him.

Struggling to keep his emotions in check, he continued to listen to the man. There wasn't much information, but he would spare nothing to root out any and all traitors in his company, and in his life.

Grant got into his car and headed home. His temper rose as each minute ticked by. If it hadn't been past midnight, he'd be at the academy or Tamara's home, demanding an explanation. There was so much wrong and unfair in this mess that his rage bounced from her betrayal to the interns' betrayal and her trickery all along. Most of all, his heart had been used. He would sit at home until the sun came up and then take matters into his own hands.

He pulled into his driveway and slammed on his brakes. Tamara's car was parked in her usual spot. He looked up at the house, noting that a few lights were on, which was not unusual. His pulse pounded now that he didn't have to wait for the confrontation.

As he entered the house, he listened for any signs that she was awake. All remained quiet on the first floor. He walked up the stairs slowly and entered his bedroom. The TV was on, but the sound was muted. She was asleep and curled up fully clothed on the bed. Her hair, loose with soft curls, fanned the pillow. He pushed back the instinct to kiss her awake.

She stirred when he dropped his keys on the bureau. "Hey," she said sleepily. She opened her arms for his embrace.

"You knew that the guys spoke with a reporter," Grant said. He wanted to snap her awake and out of that dreamy, sexy mood.

"What?" She blinked.

"I don't have time to play twenty questions with you. So I'm going to lay it on the line. You used me. I can't believe that you'd sink to using your students like pawns. You fed me all that B.S. about helping the troubled youth. You played me like a fool. Now, I know you don't need money. So what do you get out of it? What do you get out of screwing over me and the company?"

"You've got it all wrong." She reached out to him, but he brushed her hand away. Touching her now would open the wound deeper, reminding him how much he'd shared with her.

"Did you or did you not know that the guys were talking to a reporter?"

"I took care of it. I squashed it last week."

Grant couldn't believe his ears. "Last week? You knew since last week?"

"That's why I left you that day. But I took care of everything. Then we got busy. I would've told you today."

"These emails are from today." He threw the papers at her.

"I was checking in with the guys because I knew the launch would be any day. I wanted to make sure they hadn't been approached again."

"You know what, just stop. Stop!" Grant motioned for her to stand. "Put on your shoes." She complied. "I don't want to sit here and try to sort out the lies from the truth. I don't want to try and figure out if you ever felt one ounce of love for me, the way I felt about you. No strings attached—our freaking motto. That means you're free to go." During his speech, he escorted her to the front door. She didn't cry. She didn't beg him. She quietly walked to the door and stepped out.

"You're wrong, like I was once. I'm not Vanessa. I'm not playing games at the expense of your company, or at the expense of your heart."

* * *

"Tamara, can I come in?" Becky poked her head through the door.

Tamara hurriedly wiped away the tears before waving her in.

"I was checking on you."

"You don't have to whisper. I'm fine. I'm up and it's a brand-new day."

"Oh?"

"Why do you look surprised? Don't you think that I should move on with my life? I have an academy to run. I have loyal employees and good friends." She reached out and gripped Becky's hand. "So why should I feel sad?" Her heart ached as if to remind her.

"Oh."

"Is that all you have to say? Well, I'll talk for you. Why don't we have a party?"

"Party?" Becky's brow knitted.

Tamara nodded. "I'm celebrating my new lease on life."

"You're not overcoming some terminal illness."

"What's the problem?"

"You're acting too over the top." Becky sat on the edge of the bed. "Frankly, that's my job."

"It's the new me."

"Sounds a bit fake."

"Get used to it." Tamara attempted to shoo her out of the room. "I've got things to do."

"Like what?" Becky hadn't budged.

"I'm repainting my room."

Becky looked around the room and then at her. "Did

you go through some religious awakening? Where's the Tammy I know and love?"

"The Tammy you knew and loved tried living by your rules—giving up everything for true love…or G-Dragon, if the two are the same."

"Ouch. Didn't know you could be so sarcastic in the early morning. I'm a seeker, Tammy. I jump into things with both feet."

"And land on your face."

"Then I pick up, heal and try it again."

"Hmm. I think my heart will have a callus or two. And I'm fine with that."

"Now you're going to be a cold, hard witch. Doesn't suit you."

Tamara shrugged. "Keeping it real."

Becky left the room.

Tamara pulled the stack of color samples from her bedside. Her walls would be blasted with a bold color. Some of the furniture would be traded for more modern pieces. And when she was done with her room and office, then she'd move on to reinventing herself. She planned on a new hairdo, changes to her wardrobe and a few new pairs of shoes. Over time, she planned to wipe away all lasting effects of Grant Benson. Too bad she couldn't do a mind makeover, but she'd take on one challenge at a time. Whatever it took to erase the longing in her heart, she was willing to do. Her pride stung. Her body craved. Her thoughts ran traitorous messages that she should make a move to reconciliation.

"You're full of crap!" Becky slammed open her bedroom door with such force it bounced off the wall.

Tamara saw the fire blazing in Becky's eyes.

"Do you hear me?"

Tamara shrugged. "I think the neighbors heard you. What's your problem?"

"That you're wimping out. You're willing to let Grant go."

Tamara shook her hand fiercely. "I didn't *let* him go. He tossed me out like trash."

"He didn't know everything. And now he's apologized. The living room looks like a floral shop, and I'm having sneezing fits." Becky had her hands clasped as if she could plead her case.

"Why should his apology wipe away all that he said?" Tamara's voice faded, choked behind the swell of emotion caught in her chest and throat.

"He hurt you. I get that."

"No!" Tamara shouted. "You don't get it. You and your romantic ideals are willing to let men trample over your emotions. Then you bounce up and give them a second chance. I tried it, and it's not for me."

Tamara rushed to her bathroom for tissues. The tears stubbornly leaked from her eyes. She didn't want to shed any more tears over Grant.

"You're wrong," Becky said. "I do know what a broken heart feels like. I do know how living with regrets can break your spirit. No, I'm not always practical, but it's who I am and want to be."

Tamara emerged from the bathroom rubbing her nose. "You're right. We both deserve happiness, right? I love you for who you are. I promise not to take my anger out on you."

"Then take it out on me." Grant stepped into the bedroom.

"Oh…" Tamara couldn't get one thought to stream in a coherent fashion in her mind. She could only stare at the man who filled her doorway with his height.

As she gathered her thoughts to respond, she took in his appearance. His countenance shocked her. He appeared drawn, tired around the eyes. His shoulders drooped as if a burden sat on his shoulders, and his chiseled look had turned to a skinny look.

"And why are you here?" The question erupted in a breathless gush, laced with more curiosity than anger.

"I want a second chance." Grant looked over to Becky. "I wanted so much to take back what I said in anger. Becky called me—"

"Becky?" Tamara turned an accusatory gaze on her friend. The momentary buzz of something tender between them evaporated.

"I did try to contact you, several times. You wouldn't respond."

"You're darn right I wouldn't." Now her anger was stoked again. Tamara bit down on her rage to hold on to a shred of pride.

"I will leave you two to talk." Becky hugged Tamara's stiff body. "Give him a chance. I'm telling you that he's the one," she whispered into her ear.

Tamara waited until Becky had left, closing the door behind her. Then she sat in the nearby chair, farthest from where Grant stood.

"I will continue to apologize, but I want to open my heart to you." He took a deep breath. "Open it in a way that I've never done. Ever."

She remained still while her pulse pounded powerful percussive beats, as if setting her anger to its own music.

"My company was all I had in my heart. Everything revolved around that passion. I protect it like any guardian would with a ward."

Tamara heard the sincerity and knew that his passion matched what she felt about her academy.

"Then you entered my life. Not just you, but ten young men. You came with an energy that was thrilling, intoxicating and sometimes frightening. I had never met anyone who could take ownership of me." His fist hit his chest. His dark eyes blazed their message from across the room.

Tamara gulped, exhaling slowly.

"The young men. They have a place in my heart because I had never taken the time to mentor—really mentor—a group of young people who have challenged me to be humble, grateful and to put closure on my past. I kick myself every day for thinking that they would've betrayed me."

"You should," she mumbled, still out of sorts.

"I'm not perfect."

Her conscience pricked. Maybe she could learn a lesson or two. She cleared her throat.

"I have come to care for those guys and will continue my mentorship of them."

"Thank you. That means a lot."

"I would do anything to have you say a kind word to me. But I mean what I say, and I do it because it's sincere, not for your approval."

She nodded. "Every child who comes through the class is someone I respect and care for as if they were my younger sibling. I never want to count them out.

Sometimes that gets me in trouble when they haven't quite made the leap to being responsible."

"I know."

"No, you don't know." Tamara took a deep breath and exhaled to blow aside her nerves.

"Nothing you say will stop me from loving you."

"Can you love someone who you may not respect?" In Tamara's mind, the two were not inseparable. She began, "I once knew a guy named Darth Dawson, who had the academic potential and attitude to make something of himself. He'd enrolled at my college and was accepted, like any qualified student. Then the news hounds got wind that he was an ex-con who had served time for manslaughter, in a case fraught with circumstantial evidence and civil rights violations. Before long, students divided between having his admission revoked or accepting him and giving him a chance." She paused. Other than Darth's mother, she had never admitted her role or fully voiced her regret. "I was on the side of the trustees, and I wanted to protect the reputation of the university and to appease the donors who threatened to withdraw their contributions over this one person."

"What happened?" Grant had moved closer, but he correctly read her body language that she didn't want to be comforted; not yet, at least.

"Darth was kicked out. The unprecedented action created lots of debate, but it all came to a head when news of his death in a shoot-out with cops hit the campus a week later. The police ruled it suicide by cop." She shuddered. "I went to the funeral and heard his mother, his lawyer and all the advocates who hadn't given up on him when he was in the state juvenile system. I came away with a new focus, a new desire to do what I should have done all those years ago."

"I think you're being too hard on yourself." Grant took her hand and held it.

"Maybe. But ever since, I vowed to do right by him. The young men that I take under my wing may have backgrounds that often don't garner sympathy or willing hands of help. So my staff and I are there to empower them to change their lives."

Tamara looked at Grant for his reaction. If she was going to start this new chapter of her life, as Darth's mother had prompted, she had to unburden completely.

"Come, sit with me." Grant sat on the edge of the bed, patting the empty space next to him. She joined him.

He asked, "And nowhere in that story of forgiveness, sacrifice and compassion is there a place for me?"

"I can't think about us."

"Can't or won't?"

"You know what Oprah says…"

Grant held and kissed her—long and hard. He released her, breathing heavily, before looking into her face, into her soul. "I don't give a damn about Oprah. I'm standing in front of you, flesh and blood, and I want you to understand what you have in front of you." He placed her hand on his chest. "I am a man who is in love with you."

Tamara clenched her fist to block off the electric buzz as they connected. Too late. Nothing she did could deny what her body and her heart craved.

"I thought that I wanted to be a bachelor all my life. Did everything in my power to stay true to that vision."

He exhaled. "I'm not going to lie, it started out feeling like this was for me. You had Oprah, and I had Clooney as my role model." He touched her cheek, stroking its outline. "We're neither. I'm your man and you're my woman, and I'm not afraid to have you in my life, not for one second."

Tamara nodded. Her soft sniffles mixed with her laughter. "I'm not afraid, either."

Everything Grant had said was true. The time for fantasies and living in fear were over. She wanted her man, forever and ever.

* * * * *

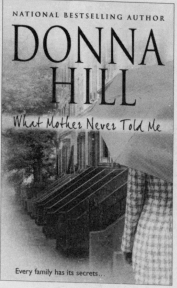

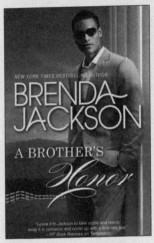

REQUEST YOUR FREE BOOKS!

2 FREE NOVELS
PLUS 2 *FREE GIFTS!*

KIMANI™
ROMANCE

Love's ultimate destination!

The newest title
in the Alexanders
of Beverly Hills
miniseries!

FIVE STAR SEDUCTION

Essence Bestselling Author
JACQUELIN THOMAS

Zaire Alexander wants to become a major force in her family-owned
chain of hotels. But the heiress has another goal for her immediate
future: seduce Tyrese Bemingham. Too bad the sexy attorney seems
just as determined to resist her. Yet when Zaire's life is threatened,
all he knows is he can't lose her…even if it means risking everything.

"[An] enjoyable read."
—RT Book Reviews on *FIVE STAR ATTRACTION*

The Alexanders of Beverly Hills

Available June 2013 wherever books are sold!

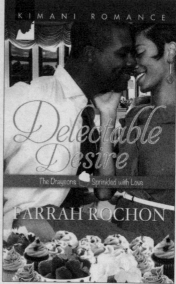

Can she overcome
the past to find
future happiness?

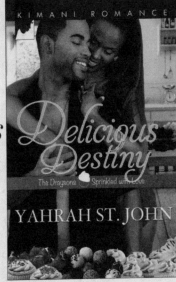

Delicious
Destiny

YAHRAH
ST. JOHN

It's been years since Shari Drayson had her heart broken. And when
Grant Robinson finally tracks her down, he doesn't expect to meet
her son—*who looks exactly like him.* Determined to claim what is his,
Grant insists they marry at once. But his bride soon realizes she's at
risk for another heartbreak. Can Grant convince her that his love is
all she needs?

**"St. John breaks the monotony of traditional
romance with this unique novel."
—*RT Book Reviews* on *DARE TO LOVE***

The Draysons  Sprinkled with Love

Available June 2013 wherever books are sold!